Realms Book 1 The Hidden Fairy

By Madam Crystal Butterfly

ISBN: 978-1-7348686-8-5

This story is intended for older teens and adults due to mature content, including profanity and sexual situations

I would like to dedicate this book to my family for always being there for me through good times and bad, and for being my number one supporters in my literary career.

Chapter 1

College

It was a sunny day in the city of St. Louis as Willow rode her bike to her aunt's art gallery. Willow was an eighteen-year-old woman with lovely brown skin and glittering chestnut eyes. As her bike glided along, her long brown braids whipped through the air, causing her to wish that she had put on the purple headband that she left on the dresser in her room. But she quickly changed her mind.

The headband clashed with her lime green tank top, and it looked awkward with her faded, ripped jeans. As she turned the corner, her mind drifted to a problem she was trying to solve earlier that day.

Harris-Stowe State University or William Jewell College? Then again, I'm ignoring Washington State University. Dammit, I got accepted by several colleges. Why is it so hard for me to pick one? But that's not even my biggest problem. I need to find a way to talk to Aunt Martha about my parents. No, dammit, just stick to the plan.

Willow's stomach growled, making her realize that she forgot to eat breakfast. She noticed she was a few blocks down from a smoothie bar where her friend worked. There was still some time before she needed to be at her aunt's gallery, so Willow headed for the smoothie bar.

When she reached the smoothie shop, she parked her bike. After chaining up her bike, Willow walked into the crowded shop. There was nothing special about the inside of the shop. It had white walls and gray tile floors and a long counter where drinks were being ordered on the right. On the wall behind the counter was a menu with the drink options. Willow walked up to the counter where her friend Darrell was working. Darrell had a shaved head, milk chocolate skin, and hazelnut eyes. He was wearing a blue shirt with the label "Smoothie World", in addition to a pair of blue jeans. When Willow walked up to him, she noticed he seemed tired.

Darrell said, "Hey, Willow, want your usual avocado, spinach, and mango smoothie? Or do you want to shake it up and try something new?"

Willow thought for a moment before looking at the menu posted on the wall behind Darrell. Thinking to herself, *"I won't be coming here for a while when summer ends. Guess I should try a few menu items I'm always thinking about trying."*

She ordered a blueberry, strawberry, ginger, and spinach smoothie. After she paid, Darrell told her that his shift was about to be over and if she sat in one of the booths, he would bring her smoothie over to her when it was ready and join her for a chat.

Willow found a booth, and once she sat down, her mind went back to picking a college. Darrell walked over with her smoothie. As he sat down across from her, she noticed he was holding a cup of coffee.

Darrell announced, "I officially don't work here anymore."

"I bet you're happy about that."

"Yes and no. I didn't like having to make drinks all day, but the manager is nice and gave me good hours. Plus, I get along with the people here."

Willow inquired, "Speaking of hours, how early did you get up? You seem tired."

"I had to get here at six this morning, but I'm tired cause my little sis had a rough night last night."

With concern in her voice, Willow asked, "What happened?"

"She caught some kind of illness. I can't think of the name of it. You know she's just a baby, and she was having trouble breathing."

"Did she have to go to the hospital?"

Darrell explained, "Thankfully, no, the pediatrician told my parents what medicine to get. It seemed to help her, but someone needed to stay up with her to monitor her breathing. My mom was going to do it, but since both my parents have to work today, I volunteered to watch my sister since my shift was just for the early morning. My grandma arrived at our house before I left for my shift here, and she's going to stay at the house all day. So, when I get home, I'll probably take a nap."

"You earned it, Mr. Princeton University."

"Speaking of college, Jamala and I broke up."

Willow's heart leaped as she asked, "Why? You two have been dating since freshmen year."

"To be honest, I didn't want to. But I'm going to Princeton, and she is going to the University of Florida. If the long-distance doesn't cause problems for us, then all the new people we will meet and want to date will."

Using a whispered tone Willow remarked, "College is going to change us."

Darrell questioned, "Have you picked one of the schools you got accepted into yet?"

"No."

"Does it have anything to do with Sandy?"

"No, why would she affect me picking a college?"

Darrell explained, "That spoiled rich girl goes out of her way to make your life hell. I get she's not happy with her dad dating your Aunt Martha, but that's no reason to go nuts on you."

Willow said, "I'm going to have to side with Vanessa about that."

"Who is Vanessa? And what are you agreeing with her about?"

"Vanessa is Sandy's younger sister. Anyway, Vanessa thinks Sandy's crazy attitude has nothing to do with my aunt being her dad's girlfriend."

"Why?"

"Well, Aunt Martha had always wanted to open her own art gallery. I believe that she is a talented painter. After finding a group of investors willing to invest in her dream of opening a gallery, she gave her two-week notice, quitting her job as Uncle Eric's secretary. At this point Uncle Eric, Sandy's father, was determined to go on a date with Aunt Martha. He had been hesitant to act on his feelings since Aunt Martha was one of his employees, fearing that she would think that he was a perv. However, now that she had given her notice and his divorce was final, he only had one other concern."

"What was he worried about?"

"He was one of the major investors in her new gallery venture. Uncle Eric didn't want my aunt to feel obligated to date him, concerned that he may change his mind about investing if she said no. I'm not sure when this happened, but apparently, he and Aunt Martha had a talk, and they acknowledged their mutual feelings for each other. They were not ready for anyone to know about the relationship, so they agreed to secretly begin dating. They kept it a secret for years, but Uncle Eric's children and I knew they were going out."

Darrell said, "I don't get how that disproves my point."

"Uncle Eric's ex-wife Yennifer, from what Sandy said, "is not a good mom."

"You believe the crazy chick."

Willow, defending Sandy, said, "She was not always a nut. Sandy used to be a cool big sister to me and her siblings. She was even close to my Aunt Martha. Anyway, Sandy told me that her mom was always angry about anything and everything. It was wise to stay out of her way because anything could set her off. Eventually Sandy's parents separated. At that point, Yennifer, Sandy's mom, took Sandy and her younger siblings and moved in with her then boyfriend. I think the guy's name was Thomas.

As the divorce negotiations proceeded, Yennifer learned that the prenuptial agreement that she signed before her marriage to Uncle Eric was airtight; she would only receive forty million dollars- no alimony and no child support. Out of spite, she dropped her children off on a random street corner somewhere on the outskirts of the city."

"Damn, so that is where Sandy gets her crazy. How did their dad find them?"

Willow continued, "Once their mom basically told them to get out of the car and drove away, Sandy realized that as the oldest she had to find a way to contact her father. After looking around she noticed that there were several houses near the corner where they had been abandoned. She chose one of the houses and knocked on the door."

Darrell, aghast, said, "Wait, you're telling me that Sandy and her siblings just went into some random stranger's house looking for help?"

Willow continued, "Yes, I am. Luckily it was a kind person who allowed Sandy to use her phone. Sandy called Uncle Eric's office; however, it was my aunt who picked them up. At this point, my Aunt Martha had just filed her two weeks' notice with Uncle Eric."

"Dude didn't want to be bothered with his kids either."

"It wasn't like that. My aunt was in the area where Sandy's mom had abandoned them, so she volunteered to get them and take them home. After Uncle Eric saw how willing Aunt Martha was to jump into this bad situation and help care for his kids, he told me that there was no way he was letting her slip away. Like I said before, his kids and I knew."

Darrell questioned, "How?"

"It was impossible for us not to notice, no matter how much Uncle Eric and my aunt tried to hide it. Growing up, my aunt and I were always at Uncle Eric's house. On most days, when we weren't at their house, they were at our house. I don't remember ever not spending the holidays with them and their extended family."

"Must have been rough having to spend a lot of time with Sandy."

Sadness in her voice, Willow acknowledged, "No, I told you, Sandy used to be like one of the best people."

"I have a hard time believing that."

"You met her when she started acting crazy. Like Vanessa, I don't know what happened to her halfway through the middle of her senior year of high school. She just got angry and mean. Then she started sneaking out to party, drink, and get high almost every night. Her dad and my aunt were worn out from chasing her around and trying to get her to straighten up."

Darrell said, "She probably was desperate to impress everyone at school."

"Maybe, but she didn't use to care what people thought of her."

"Anyone can change."

Willow acknowledged, "I guess."

"Why did her dad not send her to something like a military school?"

"She was almost out of high school, so there was no point. Even if she could have gone, I don't think she would have been able to handle a strict school environment. Uncle Eric also hates the idea of any boarding school. His parents sent him to boarding school and pretty much ignored him. Everyone thought when Sandy got into college she would calm down. We were completely wrong. But I'm not going to keep bothering myself with her issues. She has bigger fish to worry about, and I need to pick a college."

"What happened to her?"

"The last time we spoke, Uncle Eric told me that he cut her off financially; however, he doesn't want her living on the streets, so he is letting her live at home."

"Why?"

Willow, sharing information with Darrell, replied, "She dropped out of Pepper Hill, when she only had one year left to go."

Darrell said, "The party school?"

"Yep, the school put her on academic probation, and she decided to drop out in response to the news.

When Sandy dropped out of college, she expected her dad would give her money to do whatever she wanted. Her dad made it clear he was not putting up with that shit. He told her she could stay in the house, but he took away her car and credit cards, and she was on her own when it comes to food and anything else she needs."

Darrell laughed, "Shit, he won't let her use the fridge?"

"Nope, he won't even allow her to have dinner with the family. I take that back. He said he would make an exception for holiday dinners. I think he is tired of her acting like a nut. She is an adult, and he figured giving her more responsibility will get her to stop acting crazy."

"Good, that crazy witch stalked my cousin for a week after he dumped her."

"I know you're talking about your cousin, but he was cheating on her while encouraging her drug use."

"I know, it's just what she did in response was going too far."

"I understand, and I can't say you're wrong. But why did he even go out with her if he wanted to fool around with other girls?"

Darrell said, "I think he just wanted to count her as a conquest. You know he's a spoiled jackass cause my dad's mom left him all her money when she passed. I wonder if dating him is what made her think it was okay to use hard drugs."

Willow, again sharing information, said, "She was using drugs long before she met him. He just probably made things worse. Speaking of being nutty, my aunt has been acting a little strange lately."

Sarcastically, Darrell said, "Stranger than usual?"

Willow frowned as she said, "What did you say, asshole?"

Darrell apologized, "I'm sorry, that was rude. What I mean is your Aunt Martha has those moments where she goes into her own world. And it always seems to get worse when someone brings up your mom and your mom's boyfriend from what I see. But when you said she's acting strange, I assumed she has gotten worse."

"No, she just started avoiding Uncle Eric."

"Why?"

"I'm not sure. He took her to Tokyo for a week as a surprise. Since their return, she spends all of her time trying to avoid him. At first, I thought it was because he tried to get her to let him buy me a car again."

"He wants to buy you a car?"

Willow replied, "Yes, and for some reason, she is against it."

"I guess she doesn't want him getting you anything too expensive."

A perplexed Willow continued, "I would agree with you if she hadn't let Uncle Eric buy me expensive things before and send me to private school."

Darrell said, "You're eighteen, so just tell him to get you the car if he wants to."

Willow, with a smile, said, "I did, and he told me he's going to buy me a car and keep it on his property. But I had to promise to keep it a secret from Aunt Martha."

"If he's that scared of her knowing about the car, then she must be that good in bed."

Willow massaged her temple while saying, "Seriously, Darrell?!"

Apologizing, Darrell said, "Sorry, but she has him on a short leash, and he's not trying to break free."

"I know, but you don't need to say that."

"Willow, forgive me, but do you think it involves your parents?"

"Why?"

"We were just talking about how your aunt gets a little strange when your mom and her boyfriend, who may be your dad, are brought up. Remember when your aunt had an episode during parent-teacher night when we were in kindergarten? After that nosy woman, what's her name?"

"Miss Fields."

Darrell explained, "When she started pressing your aunt about your parents, your aunt started to get shaky. Then she snatched you and ran out of the room, shouting."

Willow's mind drifted to the incident Darrell spoke of. She remembered how Miss Fields walked up to her aunt, pretending to be nice, until she learned Willow's aunt was not her mom. This realization was followed by a hailstorm of questions about Willow's parents. Her aunt started to get shaky, and she refused to answer. Miss Fields suddenly got more determined to find out what happened to Willow's parents, and she started questioning her aunt asking how Martha became Willow's guardian. Almost instantly, Willow's aunt started screaming that Miss Fields was "with them."

With a look of fear in her eyes, Aunt Martha suddenly grabbed Willow up in her arms, shouted at Miss Fields as she ran out of the room, "I'm not going to let you hurt my family!" Willow remembered that her aunt was holding her so tightly as they rushed out of the building that she could barely breathe. After putting Willow in the back seat of their car, her aunt began speeding down the road until they reached their house. Again, she grabbed Willow in her arms and ran into the house."

They spent the rest of the evening at home, with all the doors and windows locked, with her aunt guarding the front door with a gun. The next day her aunt seemed to be better, but Willow was too afraid to ask about the incident from the night before. When she went back to school, Willow's teacher at the time, Miss Simon, began questioning her about her home life. Willow was frightened by her teacher's questions. This fear only got worse when a social worker started visiting their home regularly.

Thankfully, Eric Williams came to the rescue. He had donated funds for a new state of the art computer lab and funding for a greenhouse, allowing students to grow the vegetables served in the lunchroom. The social worker stopped visiting and Willow's teacher was fired. Her aunt told her Eric made the mean social worker disappear because he had invested in the art gallery, but Willow never believed that.

Willow looked at Darrell while saying, "Uncle Eric has always looked out for us. I don't understand why my aunt won't return his calls. He's been ordering paintings from the same crappy artist every day just to get her to talk to him."

Darrell guessed, "This has to be about your folks."

Willow exhaled before saying, "Why are you so stuck on that idea?"

"Come on, Willow. Your whole life if anyone even mentions anything about your parents, she freaks out. I know you don't want to believe it, but she had to have been there when your parents disappeared. Whatever happened to them must have given her PTSD or something."

"Darrell, I already suspected that years ago."

"I had a feeling you did, but that's not why I'm bringing this up. Your aunt may have her moments, but she's never been dangerous. That's probably because Mr. Williams has always been there helping out. More than that, I think you played a bigger role in helping her stay ok."

Willow agreed, "I can't argue with you about that."

Darrell continued, "Your Uncle Eric probably is scared that your aunt might have a breakdown once you go to college. Clearly, money's not a problem for him, so he probably offered to pay for the best therapy to help her. Or he offered to help find your parents."

"Why would he try to find my parents?"

"You said the only information about them you got out of your aunt is that they were taken."

"I also told you she made it clear to Uncle Eric a long time ago that she doesn't want him looking into what happened to my parents. He holds a lot of money and influence. If she does not want him involved in what happened, then it has to be really bad. She told me we left Texas because they disappeared. Looking into the situation is probably dangerous."

"From what you have told me in the past I've been questioning if the cops have ever been told that they were missing. The police may have never investigated what happened to them and possibly haven't been looking for them. Sorry if I'm reading into your situation too much. Just because she doesn't want Mr. Williams involved doesn't mean he has not already gotten involved. He probably started poking around in your parents' disappearance years ago, to give your aunt closure, and I bet, unlike the cops he found some answers, too."

"Now that you say that you may be right." Willow finished her smoothie before continuing to say, "I've suspected for a long time that my aunt knows what happened. But whenever I get the courage to ask her about it, she starts shaking and zones out for a moment."

Darrell speculated, "Whatever she saw must have been scary. Why else would she not want Mr. Williams to use his money to help?"

"Yeah, it made me come to a decision."

"What did you decide?"

"So, Uncle Eric wants me and Vanessa to take a few weeks to tour a few of the colleges where I have been accepted. She is graduating the year after next, and he also thinks it will help me decide on a college."

"OK."

"I found my aunt's old address in Texas. I talked to Vanessa about it, and we are going down there to look for clues."

Darrell, using a protective tone, said, "No, you're not."

"Excuse me?"

"I'm going with you guys, and I'm bringing my buddy Montrell with us."

"That's sweet, but…"

Darrell continued, "But nothing. You said yourself you think something messed up probably went down. There may be nothing at your aunt's old place, or there could be some nut hanging around. So, we are going with you two. Seriously, Willow, you of all people should have factored in the danger if you were bringing someone."

"Dammit, you're right."

Darrell asked, "When do you want to head out?"

Willow replied, "I'm not sure yet. Vanessa and I need to figure out how we are going to get there."

"Doesn't she have a car?"

"It's totaled."

"What?"

"Sandy stole Vanessa's keys, got plastered, and then slammed Vanessa's car into a tree."

"Shit."

"I know, and her dad hasn't bought her a new one. He wants to buy both of us a car at the same time so that he does not have to go back and forth with the dealer. Anyway, I better go. My aunt needs me to deliver a painting to Uncle Eric."

"Alright, I'll see you later."

Willow then walked out of the smoothie shop and retrieved her bike. As she peddled off, she found herself feeling a little bit better about her plan.

Chapter 2

Call Him, Dammit!!

Willow turned down the street leading to her aunt's gallery. While she rode, she reflected on her time growing up in St. Louis. It was not always easy living there, especially when they first arrived in the city. Willow was only three when she and her aunt came to the city. Her aunt literally did not have a penny to her name. All she had was a few clothes for herself and Willow and nothing else.

According to her aunt, they slept in the park for three months. Her aunt admitted to her that she had done minor shoplifting for a while to provide them with food and a tent to sleep in. They would also get washed up in a public bathroom. Whenever Willow tried to remember their life in the park, she could only vaguely remember her aunt telling her bedtime stories inside of a blue tent.

Her aunt told her that she always hated telling the story of when they came to the city because it made her feel like a failure for not having money to provide Willow with a home and warm food. Whenever Willow would ask why she had no money, it always was the same story. Her aunt would try to tell her but would then get overwhelmed with fear.

Willow thought, *I don't understand why she won't do anything about her fear. Whatever happened traumatized her, but she won't even take up Uncle Eric's offer to pay for therapy.*

Her mind then turned to the day she and her aunt first encountered Eric Williams. They were still living in the park, but her aunt had succeeded in creating a fake address for them so that she could get Willow into the new fancy preschool. The school had been built by a foundation dedicated to giving children from low-income families the best early education for free. When Willow and her aunt were leaving after registering with the school, they bumped into Eric Williams and his now ex-wife Yennifer who had just finished a meeting with the principal. Willow could not remember what they had talked about. All she knew was Eric and Yennifer were there because they were contributors to the pre-school. They wanted to see for themselves the acceptance process and meet some of the applicants.

Her aunt, looking for work, slipped into the conversation, along with the lie of how they were staying with friends. Eric mentioned he was in the market for a secretary, and her aunt said she would apply. A week went by, and she got the job. After two months, they moved into a rental house, which her Aunt Martha bought from the original owners six years ago.

Reflecting on the past, Willow wondered what was stopping her aunt from marrying Eric. It was not like he had not asked her several times. Heck, except Sandy, all his kids called her aunt mommy. One of Eric's aunts had bought the dress she proclaimed Martha would wear for the wedding. Eric's aunt would even pressure Martha to hurry up and marry her nephew so they could give her another baby to spoil.

The more she thought about family, the more she started to think about her parents. From the little bit her aunt told her about her mom and dad, Willow knew that Aunt Martha was her mom's younger sister. Her mother was married to a man who might be Willow's biological father. Her mother's husband was someone she did not marry out of love. Instead, the match was made from pressure from her mother's parents to please their business associates. Willow had a feeling from what her aunt said that her birth was more likely the result of an affair. Whenever she tried to ask more about it, her aunt would shrug, followed by her usual statement, "just be happy your mama got out of that bad deal quickly."

As a young girl Willow discovered the story behind what her aunt had referred to as a bad deal. Apparently in the middle of Willow's mother's pregnancy, her mother's husband demanded that she get an abortion. Despite her mother being too far along in her pregnancy to have abortion as an option, he told her that if she did not abort the baby, he would kill her and rip the baby from her womb and crush the fetus with a rock. It goes without saying that her mom was not a fan of the idea. Willow suspected her mother's husband did not know about the affair since the only problem he had with his wife's pregnancy was the fact the baby was a girl. Thinking about the whole situation did give Willow some joy knowing her mother's boyfriend, who was probably her real dad, wanted to protect her. Her boyfriend helped her mother sneak away from her father. Once her mother was safe, she considered getting an annulment but changed her mind. She moved in with her boyfriend and never spoke to her husband again until whatever happened to them happened. Willow had not been told this story all at once, just bits and pieces over the years, so she thought her mother's husband was why they left Texas. When Willow's aunt realized this, she quickly let Willow know she was wrong.

Unfortunately, other than that little bit of information and how they lived in Texas, her aunt could not bring herself to talk more about Willow's mom and her mother's boyfriend. There were moments when her aunt seemed to want to tell Willow more about her parents. Sadly, her aunt would barely finish a sentence before freaking out and quickly changing the subject. Willow would never press her for more information. Recalling what happened to her parents would be too much for her aunt to handle, out of fear. Despite her aunt's inability to talk about Willow's parents, Willow had tried for years to get answers on her own. However, she could never find any leads until the week her aunt was in Tokyo. Willow was cleaning the house when she tripped over a loose floorboard in the hallway. Upon inspection, she found a small box. Inside the box was a key attached to an address. There was also a note saying, "Take Willow far away. He won't hurt the rest of us. I'm sorry, Havoc, I shouldn't have trusted him."

Willow's heart leaped as she remembered the note. She thought, *so far auntie has not noticed I looked under the floorboard. I don't know who this Havoc person is, but my aunt must know him.*

She reached the outside of her aunt's art studio. The art studio was a small building connected to two other buildings. It also had a large front window with the words "Immortal Art" written in gold letters above it. After parking her bike, she went inside.

As soon as Willow entered the building, she averted her eyes in disgust because there was a large photo of a naked, severely overweight, blue man with a large sparkler in his butt.

She heard her aunt say, "Sorry, Willow."

"Aunt Martha, what the hell was that?"

"Art, supposedly. It is a photo taken by the artist Adervill McSpring. He is super popular right now."

"Why?"

Smiling, Aunt Martha replied, "No idea. His stuff is not the usual art I acquire, but his photos sell for a lot of money, especially this one."

"What is so special about that piece of crap?"

Martha remarked, "It is one of the first pieces the artist ever created. A friend of mine was able to get hold of it. I agreed to help him sell it in exchange for thirty percent of the profit. Oh, you can look now. I covered up the photo."

Willow turned her head in her aunt's direction, happy to see that a red fabric was now covering the photo. The gallery consisted of one open room with white walls. Its floors were black tile, and there was a door against the back wall leading to a room where the art was stored.

Willow's Aunt Martha made sure the covering was on the photo properly. Martha had rich brown skin and hazelnut eyes. Her curly black hair was underneath a curly flaming red wig. A pair of gold earrings hung from her ears, and she was wearing a pink dress with pink heels. To complete her look, her lips were painted bright purple.

Martha said, "Thankfully, we already have a buyer. Once the sale is finalized, I will get two hundred thousand for it."

"Does that mean you're going to move into a bigger gallery?"

"No, it is enough money to help with your college fees, and it will give me enough money to redo the living room. You know how much I hate the living room."

"Understandable. I thought that the first thing you planned to do after buying the house was to change the living room."

Martha replied, "The other rooms were more important. My gallery also needs a lot of attention. Speaking of attention, how are you doing with picking a college?"

"I still can't decide where to go."

"Maybe that's because you haven't selected a major."

"I guess it's pretty tough to decide what I want to do for the rest of my life."

Martha commented, "You don't have to pick right away. Use your first semester to figure out what you want to do. For example, my sister was an economics major; you might enjoy that. However, her boyfriend was a political science major. That might be fun."

"What was your major?"

"I took business administration. But unlike your parents, I didn't get to finish my degree."

"Why?"

Martha looked at the ground while saying, "Let's talk about that later."

Willow forced herself not to groan. Ironically, Willow preferred her aunt's averted gaze as opposed to when her aunt suddenly shook in fear.

Martha looked at Willow as she continued to say, "You know what. I've been thinking a lot about Eric's idea of you and Vanessa touring schools."

Willow asked hopefully, "Does this mean he can buy me a car?"

In a serious tone, Martha stated, "No, I better not catch the two of you pulling something sneaky either."

Willow shrugged as she said, "What do you mean?"

"Don't try to be cute, you little shit. I know Eric probably got the idea he can secretly buy you a car."

"Why do you feel he is overstepping if he gets me a car? Except for the last four months, we practically live at his house."

"I don't. My relationship with him has been in a strange place for a while. If I let him buy you something like a car, then things will get even more awkward, and I don't want you getting caught up in our mess."

Willow took a breath as she stated, "I understand."

"Alright, now I need you to drop off another copy of a painting by Ergo Kingrige."

Willow moaned as she asked, "Is it for Uncle Eric?"

"Yes."

"Auntie, you know he has been ordering the Ergo Kingrige paintings every day."

"So?"

In an exasperated tone, Willow stated, "Oh, come on. He orders art from an artist whose work he said was not decent enough to wipe a pig's butt."

Martha calmly replied, "He is probably going to donate them to some charity event."

"Not my point about Uncle Eric."

"Ok, he might be doing this because I haven't returned his calls."

"If you're not returning his calls, how is he ordering art from you?"

Martha said, "The internet. Honestly, you should have known that right away. I'll call him soon. I just need a little more time to figure out my relationship with him."

"Why? The man's been nuts for you since I was in elementary school. And an added bonus is that he's rich."

"Kiddo, getting into a relationship for money alone is not healthy."

"True, but still, he wants to spend it on you."

"Fine, I promise I will call him tomorrow."

"Good, I'm tired of driving up to his house."

"It's not that far away."

"The ride up there is not my issue. It's Sandy. Lately when I bump into her, she goes on a tirade about how we are responsible for her father not loving her."

"I don't know what to do about her. It just doesn't make any sense. Sandy was always such a kind child. She even looked out for you and her younger siblings. Now she seems to be obsessed with drugs and alcohol." Martha took a breath before continuing to say, "What happened to my sweet little girl who wanted to be an artist? She used to practically live at the gallery. She loved being near the paintings all day, especially when she was acting as a lure for her dad."

"What?"

"I thought you knew. When you kids were little and I opened the gallery, Sandy didn't stay here every day just because she loved art. Her dad told her that if she stayed late, I would have to bring her home, which would give him an excuse to invite us to dinner."

Laughing, Willow said, "Uncle Eric is sneaky."

"Kiddo, you have no idea. But I'll never be mad at him for pulling that stunt."

"We do always have fun at his place."

Martha continued, "That's not my reason. Willow, you may have been a good kid and tried to ease my burdens as best you could, but after quitting my job it took a lot of work and energy to get the gallery ready for its opening. I was exhausted everyday thanks to Eric's little scheme to get me to spend more time with him. I got to make sure you were well fed, and it saved you and me from having to help you with your science homework."

Willow smiled and said, "Can't say no to a guy whose head butler has a biochemistry degree. Anyway, give me the car keys so I can drop off the painting."

"Alright, also speaking of food, I'm cooking dinner tonight. Stop at the store and grab ten granny smith apples on your way back."

"OK."

Just then the door opened, and a woman walked in. At the sight of the woman, Willow's heart raced as Martha glared at the woman with a murderous gaze.

The woman had dyed her long silky hair a bleached blond color. Her skin was a rich hazel brown while her eyes were emerald green. She had a small white crystal nose ring, and her red painted lips were formed into an unwelcoming smile. The woman wore a black cocktail dress and red high heels.

Martha snapped, "Yennifer, what the literal fuck are you doing in my gallery?"

Yennifer replied, "Temper, temper- Martha, I haven't done anything to make you a bitter bitch. I'm just about to have a romantic evening with my husband. I wanted to thank you for ending that silly affair you were having with him. It was clearly inevitable that he would come back to me, his wife, anyway. But it's good of you to have faced reality and ended the affair. Now I can focus on healing the wounds that your affair caused in my household."

Willow felt more than a little dumbfounded by what Yennifer said. Yennifer and her uncle had been divorced for several years. He hated her presence and told Willow he would rather get tuberculosis than ever be married to her again.

Martha replied, "You are a sad woman. It's bad enough you treat your children worse than garbage. But you hold on to this idea that the man who divorced you because you had an affair, wants you back."

Yennifer snapped, "He does want me back! You just need to understand you have no business with him. Stay away from my family!"

She turned and stormed out of the gallery, and Martha said, "I need a beer."

Willow replied, "You always say that when you talk to her."

"Talking to that bitch always makes me crave a cold beer."

"You think she showed up to keep you from calling uncle?"

Martha stated, "I know she did. Yennifer probably snuck into Eric's house again and heard that he and I were having issues. She must have guessed this was the perfect time to try to get him back."

Willow said, "He's not dumb enough to go back to a woman who wants him for his money. Knowing uncle, he would rather jump into a shark pit than go back to her."

Martha stated, "If she's sulking around him, then I should take it as a sign to go ahead and call him. Poor Eric is most likely stressed from dealing with her and needs someone to talk to."

Willow added, "You are the only one he really opens up to about the stress she causes him. Although she did throw me off when she said they were going to have a romantic night."

"Willow, a romantic night means he has to talk to her about their kids. It's probably about Pete because the camp he wants to go to is demanding to speak with her. I'm not sure why because Eric has full custody, so they don't need approval from both parents. Anyway, the issue with the camp will be over soon, since I've decided I don't want him to go."

"Why?"

Martha announced, "I don't trust summer camps, and I don't like the idea of spending the whole summer away from one of my kids."

Willow wanted to know, "Why don't you trust camps?"

"I've heard too many stories about camp bullying, and I don't like him being in a place where I can't get to him quickly if he needs me."

"Fair point, but he does really want to go."

Martha stated, "He'll change his mind about going to science camp once I tell him I found a summer science program he'll like better, right here in town."

"If you say so. I better go deliver that art."

"Alright, drive safe."

After retrieving the painting from the back room, then making sure it was secure in the back of the car, Willow hopped into the driver's seat of her aunt's blue truck. As she cranked up the engine, she questioned her aunt's behavior. For as long as she knew, her aunt had moments when she was a little off. But now, she felt like she was trying to cover something up.

As she drove the car onto the road, Willow tried to forget about the whole incident with Yennifer. But her mind replaced thoughts of Yennifer by replaying what her aunt said about not finishing her degree. As she got on the road, her mind was buzzing with questions. *I wonder if Aunt Martha was in school when they vanished. It would explain why she did not finish. She also seemed nervous when she told me she had dropped out.*

Willow turned the corner when her thoughts turned to the Williams family. She did not want to run into Sandy, especially after dealing with Yennifer. It was not because Sandy was going to insult her. It was more about how she and Sandy used to be friends. She just could never understand why one day Sandy spiraled out of control.

She pulled up to the gate that led inside the Williams community. The security guard recognized her and waved her in without question. As Willow drove into the neighborhood, she fell into her habit of admiring all the houses as she drove by.

Eventually, she pulled up to the Williams estate. The home had a tan brick driveway where a red sports car and a pink truck were parked. Meanwhile, the lawn was home to three large cherry trees that sat in the center. The house was a light beige with a Spanish style roof. There was a patio in the front of the house, and it was decorated with hanging baskets full of purple petunias. There were also a few white rocking chairs sitting beside the black steel door that covered the glass door that led into the house.

She parked her aunt's car near the front entrance. Willow immediately got out of the car only to be met by Vanessa. Vanessa was a tall girl with curly brown crochet braids. Her skin was a smooth milk chocolate, while her eyes were a glittering hazelnut. Vanessa was wearing a simple red T-shirt, jeans and pink tennis shoes.

Vanessa said, "Hey Willow, my dad told me to tell you just to drop the art in front of the front door. One of the maids is going to take it to the basement."

Willow inquired, "Why does he want it in there?"

"To keep the paintings out of sight until he can set up a charity auction."

"He really was trying to set up an auction."

"What do you mean?"

"I thought he was just buying a bunch of paintings in hopes of talking to my aunt."

Vanessa confirmed Martha's theory and said, "He was, and the whole charity auction thing is just his way of disposing of the art."

Thoughtfully, Willow said, "Makes sense."

"Do you want to come in?"

"No offense, but I don't want to bump into Sandy."

"I more than understand. She came in super late last night and refuses to let herself sleep."

"That's just weird."

Vanessa, with sadness in her voice, continued, "I know, right now, she is in her room blasting music to keep herself awake. My dad told the staff if she did not go to sleep in thirty minutes to bust in her room and take her music away."

"I think it might be wiser to call a doctor."

"I get where you're coming from. But this is the fourth time this month she's done this. The crazy usually stops after she passes out."

Willow questioned, "Any idea why she keeps doing the weird music thing?"

Vanessa answered, "Nope, but I'm gonna find out."

Willow replied, "Good luck."

"Speaking of luck, everything good to go with our trip?"

Willow answered, "Yep, Aunt Martha doesn't suspect a thing."

"Why aren't we just having my dad look into it?"

Willow said, "Remember, Martha is against him having anything to do with my family and Texas."

"Oh right, I don't know why I forgot. I wonder why that is?"

"Your guess is as good as mine, since she won't tell us the reason."

Vanessa questioned, "Maybe he already knows what happened and wants to stay quiet."

"I've suspected that, but I don't know."

"So, are you going to talk to my dad about car shopping?"

Willow answered, "Yeah, but I'm thinking we may still want to get a rental."

"Why?"

Willow shares new information with Vanessa. "We agreed that someone involved with whatever happened to my parents might be at the address I found. Since it might be dangerous, my friend Darrell and one of his friends, Montrell, will be coming with us."

"That's a good idea. We should have thought of that first. Want to go to the rental place tomorrow?"

"Let's do it the day after tomorrow. I need to come up with an excuse to tell your dad. He's been excited about me taking a trip in my first car."

"Good point. Oh, has mommy changed her mind about letting dad get you a car?"

Willow stated, "No, she is also suspicious he will get me a car anyway. I'm not going to stress about it. Cause I'm more worried about her calling him. I doubt she wants to end things with him, but she is being too weird about talking to him."

"She's getting all worked up about dad wanting her to move in."

"Wait, that's what this is about?"

Vanessa confirms, "Yep, since dad can't get mommy to marry him, he's trying to get her to move into the mansion. He figured since you're going to college, she should live with us. I take that back. He's just looking for an excuse to get her to move in."

"She is planning to finally re-do the living room. She'll use that as an excuse not to move in."

Vanessa laughs, "Thank heavens your living room is just painful to look at. How you have lived with bright lime green walls is...."

At that moment Eric Williams bolted through the front door. Eric was a tall man with short curly black hair. His skin was smooth dark chocolate, while his eyes were a lovely auburn. He was wearing a dark blue suit and tie with black leather shoes.

He quickly said, "Hello, girls." Quickly jumping into his red sports car before either Willow or Vanessa could blink, the car bolted off the property and down the street.

As they stared in disbelief, Willow said, "I think she called."

Vanessa stated, "Good I need the drama with them to stop. I can't take their crazy and Sandy's crazy at the same time."

After they got the painting out of the car and put it next to the door, Willow pulled out her keys while saying, "Ok. I'm going to head out."

Vanessa, waving good bye, said, "Alright, see you later."

"Ok, bye." Willow got back into the car and started to drive off.

Chapter 3

I need to clear my head

Willow was headed to the checkout with more than just the apples her aunt wanted. While shopping she realized the encounter with Yennifer had bothered her more than she thought. This did not surprise her, knowing Yennifer had done things to traumatize her in the past. Not to mention questions about her parents were also weighing on her brain. So, she used some of the money she had saved up to load up on ice cream and other snack foods. She planned to have a pig out feast to calm her nerves. Before she reached the checkout, she heard her phone ring. When she checked it, she realized her aunt was calling.

When she answered her aunt said, "Willow, did you get the apples?"

"I'm headed to the checkout with them now."

"Good, the Williams are joining us for dinner."

"I guess that's confirmation that you and Uncle Eric patched things up."

"Yes, we did. Oh, also I took your bike home. I've already started on dinner so Sandy can take some food home."

"Sandy's coming?"

Martha answered, "Oh crap, I forgot to tell you. I called Sandy and asked if she wanted me to pack her a plate to pick up. She is on her way."

"Why?"

"Willow, I know you and Sandy don't get along right now, but I practically raised that girl, just like you, Vanessa and Peter. I'm not about to let any of my children go hungry."

"What about Uncle Eric?"

"I don't give a shit. His tough-love approach is fine, but not letting her have food is too much."

"Ok, I hope I don't bump into her when I get to the house."

"She seemed to have toned down her attitude quite a bit when I spoke to her."

Willow replied, "Probably because she wanted dinner."

"I don't know, Willow. Something in me tells me she's trying to do better."

Willow said, "If you say so. Anyway, I just checked out. I'm going to head home."

"Ok, love you, see you soon."

"I love you, too, Auntie. Bye."

After walking out of the store, Willow, trying to think of ways to delay her arrival at home to avoid seeing Sandy, decided to stop at the gas station for a soda. She had not purchased one at the grocery store and realized she would need something to wash down her junk food feast later this evening. After making her purchases and cranking up her car, Willow paused for a moment as her thoughts turned to Sandy. *Why did she have to become so mean? She was like my big sister. Her turning into the biggest bitch just doesn't make sense.*

Willow also remembered why she had not eaten dinner recently with the Williams. It had nothing to do with Sandy, but with Uncle Eric and her aunt's situation. Her aunt had been distracted by the gallery, so Willow had the house to herself.

Willow owned up to the fact that her aunt was occupied with work and out of the house, giving Willow the opportunity to hang out with friends. Once summer was over, she was not going to see them for a long time.

She drove into her neighborhood. After a few minutes, Willow pulled up into her driveway. Her house was a two-level brick home with black shutters, a blue front door, black roof, and a chimney sticking out of the top. The house was just a standard suburban home.

No sooner had she pulled up to the house than she noticed her bike parked next to the front entrance. Willow groaned while thinking, *why does my aunt always forget to bring my bike inside?*

When she jumped out to put her bike back, she heard Sandy's voice. Willow thought, *I hoped Sandy was just going to grab the food and go. I wonder who she's talking to.*

Willow could tell Sandy's voice was coming from the side of the house. She went to listen in on Sandy's conversation. Once she was a little closer, she realized that Sandy was talking to someone on her cell phone, She heard Sandy say, "I'm not doing that. I don't care if it's important to him. I know, but still, this is wrong."

Willow thought, *is someone trying to get her involved in something bad? Why does she hang out with people like that?*

Sandy continued to say, "You know you're the one person in the world who should never ask me things like this. If you take it, I'm telling dad. Oh, trust me he will believe me. He's my dad, that's why."

After that, Willow figured Sandy was done talking to whoever it was. She raced over to her bike to pretend she had just got home. Willow started to move her bike towards the garage as Sandy came out from the side of the house. Sandy had smooth dark chocolate brown skin. Her long curly brown hair was tied into a ponytail. Sandy's hazelnut eyes looked bloodshot while her lips were painted red. She was wearing a green T-shirt and a pair of ripped jeans. She was also holding a grocery bag while pulling her green bike.

She glared at Willow while saying, "I didn't hear the car pull up."

"Oh, really? I just pulled up," replied Willow.

Sandy paused before saying, "Whatever, I'm going to take this garbage your aunt shoved on me home."

"Seriously? She went out of her way to give you food. Seeing how messed up you look, you should be grateful."

"Whatever."

Before Willow could respond, Sandy jumped on her bike and sped off. Willow stamped her foot. She felt like screaming something at Sandy before she got too far. Not wanting to dwell on the matter until she could talk to her aunt about it, she also decided not to tell anyone about Sandy's phone call. Willow pulled her bike into the garage, putting it in its usual place. She decided that whatever Sandy had gotten herself into was Sandy's business and had nothing to do with her.

After putting her bike away, she proceeded to get back in the car so she could park it in the garage. After she parked and climbed out of the car, her aunt came into the garage.

Martha smiled as she said, "I thought I heard you come in. I hope you're hungry. I made pepper steak."

Willow, beginning to answer, "Sounds good. I just saw Sandy and...."

Interrupting Willow, Martha said, "Tell me about it inside. I need to finish getting things ready."

Willow gave her aunt the apples. The two of them went inside, and Willow decided not to tell her aunt about Sandy's conversation. At least until after dinner and Eric was there to hear it.

Martha asked, "Why did you buy popcorn and all this junk food?"

"I'm going to watch some movies later."

"Ok, just don't eat all of it. I'll probably want some later."

"That's why I got so much. Did you and uncle talk?"

Not answering, Martha asked, "Did you and Sandy have a pleasant chat? She was happy when I gave her food for the week. Her eyes lit up when she saw that pepper steak. I was hoping it would get her to dial back her attitude. Come and help me get the table set. Company should be here soon."

Willow headed through the garage door into the kitchen. The main level of Willow's home was open concept. The kitchen had white walls and the floors for the entire main area where a gray wood. All the kitchen appliances were stainless steel, and the countertops were made of a light gray marble. The kitchen table was white with a vase filled with pink tulips in the center. Next to the kitchen was the living room. The living room had an old orange couch that although clean, had definitely seen better days. One of the feet was broken, and there was a small cut on the left arm.

Worse, the living room floor was the only part of the house where the floors were different. They were a mossy brown and looked worn down. Not being able to afford it, Willow's aunt never changed the floors in the living room to match the rest of the house. Eric had volunteered to pay for it, but Martha would never allow him to. Her refusal also led to the walls of the living room looking awful. They were covered with fading lime green wallpaper with pink and purple wildflowers all over it. It was also peeling in a few spots, revealing a pink wallpaper underneath. There was one large window on the left wall covered by a white curtain.

On the other side of the kitchen area were the stairs leading to the upper part of the house. There was nothing special about the stairs other than their being made from the same gray wood as most of the house. Martha had her pie crust ready along with a blue plastic bowl of cinnamon strudel for the top of the pie. As she started to cut up the apples, she said, "Eric and I had a long talk about our relationship. We came to a decision."

Willow asked, "About what?"

"We can talk about it at dinner."

A little bit later, Willow finished setting the dinner table. No sooner did Willow finish the last place setting than the Williams family arrived. Eric opened the front door. Right behind him was his son Pete. Pete was a sixteen-year-old young man. He looked like a complete photocopy of his father except for his hair, which was braided into cornrows. He was wearing a loose black T-shirt, baggy black pants, and tennis shoes. Vanessa was behind him. She had changed into a casual pink dress.

A smiling Eric looked at Martha. He rushed over to kiss her. Willow was happy to see that Eric and her aunt had worked things out.

Eric, who had his arms wrapped around Martha, said "Let's tell them the good news."

Martha replied, "I need to get dinner on the table."

Eric insisted, "But I want the kids to hear our good news."

Martha stopped him, saying, "Food first, then news."

Willow, who had just put a salad on the table, said, "Vanessa and I will put the food on the table. Why not go ahead and tell us?"

Eric started telling Martha he wouldn't let her go until they broke the news. Martha giggled while saying, "Alright, alright. Eric talked me into selling this house, meaning nothing is stopping me from moving into his house."

Willow smiled as Peter said, "Finally! I don't know why you didn't move in with us a long time ago. The bulk of your clothes are in Dad's closet, and Willow's room at our place has most of her stuff."

Martha freed herself from Eric's grasp. She looked at Peter while replying, "Peter, sometimes things are complicated."

"Mommy, the only complicated thing we have to deal with is Sandy."

Vanessa put the last dish on the table while saying, "Daddy, can we please move her into the ranch house?"

Eric frowned and replied, "Young lady, for the last time, I am not throwing your sister out."

Vanessa, justifying her remarks, stated, "I'm not trying to throw her off the property, just out of the main house."

Eric explained, "Vanessa, you probably forgot about this because we keep our horses at the ranch and throw parties there, but your mother owns the ranch- not me."

Vanessa replied, "No she doesn't."

"I'm talking about Yennifer; she got it as a result of our prenuptial agreement."

"Why did you agree to give it to her in the prenup?"

"It was your late grandfather's decision. He knew I didn't like Yennifer, and as soon as he was gone, he couldn't use his influence to keep me from leaving her. Your grandfather knew I didn't want the property split up, so he assumed that if he made the ranch hers, I would never leave her if we separated. So…"

Martha said, "Can we stop talking about her? I told you that woman had the nerve to show up at the gallery today. Just dealing with her for a few minutes made me want to drink. Poor Willow is having a junk food movie night just to destress from the whole encounter."

Eric looked at Willow and asked, "Did you buy the jumbo bag of popcorn?"

"Yes," answered Willow.

"Good. I'm probably going to want some later."

"Uncle, I always buy the jumbo bag because you and auntie always want popcorn when we have it."

Vanessa said, "I have just one more question, Daddy. Why don't you buy the ranch? Then that woman will leave, and Sandy can use the Ranch as an apartment."

Eric answered, "Yennifer refuses to sell it to me. She has some bewildering idea I will get back with her if she keeps it."

Vanessa sat down at the table as she said, "Why does Yennifer ruin everything?"

Willow thought about how Eric's ex-wife was worse than Sandy ever could be. She always went out of her way to try and mess up Eric's relationship with her aunt. However, when it came to the Yennifer problem, Willow's aunt did not hate her because she interfered with her relationship. It was how easily she abandoned her children that invoked Martha's rage.

Martha said, "Let's not talk about her. Everybody, sit down so we can eat before our dinner gets cold."

After everyone started eating, Eric said, "Willow, Martha and I talked. She's agreed to let me buy you a car. So, let's head over to the dealership tomorrow."

Willow thought, *crap! I want the car, but I need that rental.*

Willow swallowed a piece of salad before excitedly saying, "Yep, yep- sounds good to me! But I was thinking that Vanessa and I should take a rental car for our trip."

Eric raised an eyebrow asking, "Why? I'm getting you a brand-new car."

Willow, attempting to justify her request saying, "It's just, it's going to take a while before I get the tag. People will be able to see the car is new."

Martha said, "She has a point."

Eric asked, "About what?"

"Eric, you know there are people who like to dent new cars. It's bad enough to avoid that problem in your own town. You know it will be worse if she's driving around out of state. And let's state the obvious driving while black."

Eric responded, "Alright, you have a point. Ok, Willow, why don't I buy you a car when you two return from your trip?"

Willow got out of her chair and went and hugged Eric's neck and said, "Thank you. I really appreciate this!"

Eric, smiling and patting her on her hand saying, "You're welcome kid."

Yes! Willow thought.

Vanessa asked, "Willow, when do you want to leave anyway?"

Willow answered, "I thought we can head out in two days. We're going to check out three schools. One is in Kentucky, and the other two are in Tennessee."

Pete asked, "Why aren't you visiting any schools here in Missouri?"

"I already went to the in-state schools I got accepted to with Aunt Martha."

Pete said, "I forgot about that. Are you, wait, is that apple pie I smell?"

Martha smiled as she said, "Yes, it is, and I've got some vanilla ice cream in the freezer."

Peter said, "Mommy, you know that is my one weakness." He frowned as he said, "Unlike Yennifer."

In a calm tone, Eric said, "Peter, don't worry about her right now."

Martha frowned as she said, "If I hear that woman's name one more time I may scream."

Willow knew the second the words "That woman," escaped her aunt's lips, she was pissed. It was always a debate whether it was Eric or Martha who hated Eric's ex more. Eric always seemed to carry around unquestioned rage whenever he heard from or saw Yennifer. But Martha would be triggered so severely by the sight of Yennifer that she sometimes would fall into a blind rage and attack her if provoked.

Martha continued to say, "I thought when I saw that witch earlier, she was just trying to piss me off. But two of my kids even wanting to bring up that bitch's name in my presence is odd."

She's correct. None of Uncle Eric's children like to talk about their biological mother.

Eric took a breath before saying, "I had to talk to her earlier because Pete does not want to go to that camp anymore. We heard about a summer program in the city he's more interested in."

Martha said, “Good, I heard about that and wanted to talk to you about it.”

Eric continued “When I talked to her, she somehow had heard that you and I weren’t speaking. So, she got the idea that she could talk me into going out with her. She even demanded I take her to a fancy dinner tonight. The two of us got into a huge argument when I said no, and she threatened to mess up the gallery if I did not go out with her. Sadly, the kids heard me yelling at her.

Pete and Vanessa got worried that I was arguing with you for some reason, which stressed them out. I let them know I was not yelling at you, but the whole thing stressed us all out for a bit.”

In a stern tone, Martha said, “I’m guessing that’s when she got the idea to head over to the gallery. I admit I should not have gone five days without talking to you. But what possessed her to think she still had a chance with you?”

Eric shrugged as he said, “I don’t know how her brain works. The only way she could have learned about our troubles is if she snuck into the house and spied on me. My security team is still trying to figure out how she got into the main house. They have been good at keeping her out all year.”

Martha questioned, “You didn’t let her in?”

Eric responded, “Martha, you know how upset I get when she sets foot near me. Worse than that, she upsets Vanessa and Pete. Apparently, she also called them both a few days ago. She told them some crap that she and I were getting re-married, so they needed to move out of the house by the end of the week. She doesn’t even understand that they are still kids; where does she expect them to go? Then again, she doesn't understand that I want nothing to do with her either. Anyway, I don't want to talk about her anymore. We were having a nice time until she was brought up."

Martha's face softened as she said, "You're right, my goodness, that woman just reminds me so much of my mother."

The second Martha mentioned Willow's grandmother, her heart raced. Martha had never talked about Willow's grandparents outside of the one-story she told her about her mom.

Before Willow tried to ask how her grandparents were like Yennifer, Peter said, "How is Yennifer like your mom? You're not crazy."

Martha got up from the table while saying, "I need a little wine. Eric, would you like a glass?"

Eric said, "No, I'm driving."

As Martha retrieved a bottle of Merlot from the fridge, she said, "Yennifer has her attitude. She is just nasty and mean like both my parents."

She started to pour herself a small glass of wine as Willow hung on every word. Martha continued, "They practically exploded when I wanted to go to college. I had to earn a scholarship to go to school because unlike my sister, they vowed not to spend one dime on my education."

Eric said, "Honey, are you sure you want to talk about this?"

Martha continued, "Yeah, I know, I know I have my freak-outs, but it's past time for me to tell Willow what monsters her grandparents are, especially when they played a big role in our move to Texas."

Willow thought, *we moved to Texas then moved again. Did they do something to my parents?*

Martha sat down and took a sip of wine. After which, she took a breath before continuing, "My big sister she, she."

Martha froze for a moment, and Willow felt her heart sink. She had seen this before and knew Martha wouldn't finish her story. Eric suggested they change the subject. Surprisingly, Martha wanted to continue.

Martha put her glass of wine down before saying, "Willow, your mother did everything in her power to help me get into school. But my last semester, my parents were able to succeed in getting me to drop out."

"Why?" Vanessa asked.

"Let's just say my parents have a kind of successful business. It took them longer than they thought, but they gained some influence over the heads of m..."

Martha suddenly started shaking. Her aunt's possible PTSD made Willow feel this discussion was over. Surprisingly, Martha regained her composure. She said, "My parents got me kicked out of college. When that happened, my sister became more defiant."

Willow said, "I thought she was already defiant when she helped you get into school."

"Yes and no, you see, my parents bet I couldn't go to university without their help. So, when I almost finished, they got pissed. They forced me out of school, and your mom stopped doing what our parents wanted. Instead, she did things like stop meeting with men our parents wanted her to meet, and started chasing after a guy she had a crush on for the longest time.

This was a relief to me because she would always cry about never knowing if he liked her. That and the men our parents wanted her to date were so bad there is no horrible word in any language that could describe them."

Willow asked, "Is this the guy you said my mom left her husband for?"

"Yep, but in all fairness, she was dating your possible father before my parents got her to marry that …"

Martha started to shake even worse than she had earlier. Eric stood up and walked over to Martha. He told her not to force herself to continue. In response, tears began to flow from Martha's eyes.

Martha said, "I'm sorry, I thought I, I…."

Willow said, "It's alright, Auntie. Don't be so hard on yourself."

Eric helped Martha up the stairs. As Willow's hope of learning more about her past from her aunt fizzled, she finished her dinner, before helping the others clean up. Once they got everything put away, Willow took the pie out of the oven. After sitting it on the windowsill to cool, she sat down at the table.

Pete, who had just finished washing dishes, said, "That was weird."

In a tired voice, Vanessa said, "What are you talking about? Mommy always gets weird like that when she talks about her past."

Pete added, "I know, but she usually only tries to talk to Willow about that stuff alone. I'm getting a feeling that she forced herself to tell us about that because she is worried about Willow's grandparents."

Just then, they heard Eric say, "Son, I think you're right."

They all looked at Eric as he continued, "Willow, earlier your aunt told me your grandparents contacted her this morning. They wanted to talk to you. Your aunt, however, doesn't want you to talk to them."

Willow asked, "Is it because they made her leave school?"

Eric continued, “I don’t know what it is. Martha froze up when she tried to tell me. I think she was trying to talk about them because they may be involved in something. I’m not sure why or what.”

“Do you think it has to do with my parents’ disappearance?”

“I suspect so. Martha must have tried to talk about them to all of us to try to warn us not to speak with them.”

Vanessa said, “Why would Willow’s grandparents want to talk to us”?

Eric answered, “I’m not sure. Martha tried to tell me when we got upstairs, but the shaking and inability to speak became much worse than it was before we went upstairs. I’m worried her attempt to open up about her past was too much for her. It may be a little while before she is back to her usual self. I suspect Willow’s grandparents suddenly contacting her triggered all of this.”

Willow said, “I guess that makes sense.”

“Vanessa and Pete, I called Felicia and asked her to take the two of you home. I’m staying the night to make sure Martha will be alright.”

Willow asked, “How bad is she?”

“She seems pretty upset. I got her to lie in bed to try and relax. I’m going to….”

Suddenly the doorbell rang. Eric went to answer it. The second he opened the door, Willow heard him say, “That was fast.”

Willow recognized Felicia’s voice as she heard her say, “I was nearby.”

Felicia Rochester was a tall woman with dark brown skin. Her eyes sparkled like emeralds and her thick black hair was tied into a bun. She was wearing a black suit and black leather shoes.

Felicia handed Eric the bag she was holding. She said, "I grabbed some soothing green tea for Martha. Steep it for three minutes and not one second extra. There are also some calming lavender incense and a disc with the soothing sounds of dolphins."

Eric asked, "Do I really need to use the dolphin cd?"

Felicia stated, "Must I remind you that when Martha had that horrible breakdown two years ago it was the sound of dolphins that brought Martha out of a bad state?"

Eric said, "Fair point. When did you have time to grab all of this?"

"I have emergency bags of items that help Martha in my car. Make sure to have her up and ready in three days."

"Why are you putting me on a timer?"

In a no-nonsense tone Felicia stated, "My son needs the two of you to help him open his fourth restaurant. Martha promised to supply him with art, and you promised to boost his marketing. He needs the both of you to get started before the week is out."

"I can help Thomas with his marketing from here. His place doesn't open until the end of the month. There is plenty of time to find another art dealer."

In a stern tone Felicia stated, "Eric Alexander Williams, I said you have three days, and I mean, three days. You don't want to know what I will do if you fail."

Willow tried not to giggle when Felicia gave Eric an ultimatum. It was funny how she was the only person who could intimidate him. Felicia turned her attention to Willow. She smiled at Willow while saying, "Hello Willow, how have you been doing?"

"I'm good," replied Willow.

"Good, have you picked a college?"

Willow answered, "I'm still trying to make up my mind. But I'm going to head out on a trip to see a few of the schools I was accepted to. I think I will be able to make up my mind after that."

"Vanessa mentioned to me the two of you were going on a trip. When are you going on this trip?"

"I think we will leave in two days."

"Alright, I expect you to be back before Anderson's new restaurant opens. I also expect you to have chosen an institution of higher learning by the time you return."

Using an obedient tone Willow answered, "Don't worry, Miss Felicia, I will."

"That's what I want to hear. Vanessa, Pete, I hope the two of you are ready to go. I've got a movie to get to later."

Pete grabbed the apple pie as he said, "Yep."

Eric frowned as he said, "Son, you cannot take the whole pie. Cut a slice for yourself and your sister, and Felicia."

"What about the ice cream?"

"We have cinnamon ice cream at home."

"I really wanted the vanilla."

In a frustrated tone Vanessa said, "I will go buy some later."

Felicia said, "Don't worry, I will call the house and the vanilla ice cream will be at the mansion before we arrive.

Pete cut half the pie and placed it on a plate and wrapped it with foil, then announced, "Let's go."

Willow was sitting in the living room trying to digest the information she had received from her aunt and uncle earlier. As her mind buzzed with questions, she felt herself becoming frustrated. Suddenly she felt a hand on her shoulder, making her jump. Her heart beat quickly as she turned her head to the left to discover whose hand was on her shoulder. When she realized it was Eric, she calmed down.

Eric removed his hand from her shoulder and said, "Sorry. I didn't mean to shock you. Is what Martha said bothering you?"

Willow answered, "Yeah, she never really says much about our family. Now she's telling me that I have evil grandparents."

"That news shocked me, too. I'm hoping when she gathers her nerves, she will be able to open up about what she wanted to tell us."

Willow answered, "Maybe."

Eric suggested, "You know this has been a trying day. It's still daylight outside. Why don't you head to the park for a bit? The fresh air might help you relax."

"I think you're right."

As Willow stood up, Eric said, "Willow, I have you blocked in, so just take my car."

Willow smiled as she said, "Really?"

"Yep, but if I see so much of a scratch on it, not even God will be able to save you."

Willow laughed, "Noted. Thanks, Uncle Eric."

“No problem, kid. By the way, don’t stay out too late.”

“Don’t worry, I won’t.”

Chapter 4

What the Heck?

Willow couldn't help but smile as she zoomed through the streets in Eric's red sports car. Part of her considered ditching the park. Eric rarely ever let Willow or his children near one of his sports cars, especially the red one. However, Eric would always be in the car with them. For him to let Willow drive it unchaperoned felt like a dream.

She entertained the idea of stopping at a friend's place. The idea was struck down just as quickly as it entered her mind. Knowing her friends would beg her nonstop to let them drive Eric's car, which she would never do because it wasn't her car. She also acknowledged she was still a little stressed, which made her feel that maybe it would be better to go to the park alone as she had originally planned.

When she reached the park, it took her a few minutes to find a parking space. After parking the car, her heart jumped the second she stepped out. Immediately she spotted Sandy's bike.

Willow thought, *What the hell is she doing here? Whatever, the park is a big place. I probably won't run into her.*

She locked the car before she entered the park. As Willow walked, she thought, *Auntie seemed to want to tell me something. Seeing how badly she reacted as usual; I shouldn't expect her to tell me anything else. I wish she didn't get scared like that. Stop, I can wish all I want. Whatever happened to my family must have been horrible. Now I have a strong feeling that my grandparents may have been involved.*

Willow came across a bench and decided to sit down. She sat in silence for a few minutes before thinking, *why, why are my so-called grandparents trying to talk to me now? Maybe I should at least hear them out. I'm just learning about them for the first time out of nowhere.*

They may even be willing to tell me what Aunt Martha can't. It might even make it so I don't have to go to Texas for answers. Contacting my grandparents may be easier said than done. I don't even know their names. Shit, I don't even know my parents' names!

Suddenly Willow heard a woman scream. Quickly she pulled her cellphone out of her pocket as she raced to see what was going on. She headed toward a woodsy part of the park where the shouting was the loudest. Her heartbeat intensified as she got closer to the screaming sound.

What am I doing? If I get too close, whoever is attacking her might see me and try to hurt me. Just call the cops and tell them what's going on. Then head home.

Despite the speech she gave herself, she still headed in the direction of the screaming while she dialed 9-1-1. When she reached the spot where the noise was coming from, her whole body froze, for her eyes bore witness to a fairy battling a troll. At least she thought it was a fairy battling a troll, since the only place she had seen these mythological creatures was in movies.

The troll was as large as a gorilla. His skin was wrinkly orange, and he had large faded emerald eyes. The troll's ears were almost as pointy as the creature's razor-sharp teeth. At the same time, its sharp nose looked as if it had been broken several times. It was wearing a shirt and pants that appeared to be made out of a burlap sack.

The fairy was a female with large yellow and red wings. She had smooth dark chocolate skin and glittering hazelnut eyes. At the same time, her long brown hair was full of thick curls. She held a long white staff that housed a large orange stone at the top. The fairy had on a pink crop top, blue jeans shorts, and pink tennis shoes.

Willow regained her composure. She dived behind a nearby tree. Her whole body trembled as she poked her head out to see what was going on. The fairy shot what looked like a tiny orb of light out of her staff at the troll. The monster dodged it and laughed at her.

He said, "Give it up, Princess Luna. Just had over the staff, and I promise to make your death quick."

Luna snapped, "Fuck you, asshole."

Willow thought *what kind of shit have I jumped into?*

Luna shot more tiny light orbs at the troll. A single orb hit the troll, and he flew back screaming. When that happened, Willow thought the fight was over. Luna started to shoot more orbs of light at the troll, but he quickly rolled out of the way. Before Willow could blink, the troll somehow grabbed the fairy by the leg and slammed her on to the ground. He proceeded to slam her on the ground again and again.

When the troll finally stopped, Luna had dropped her staff. Luna was very bruised and bloody as she attempted to grab her staff. The troll quickly grabbed her leg again and slammed her against the ground so hard it damaged her wings.

Willow tried to think of a way to sneak away to get help. Suddenly the troll slammed Luna against a tree. Willow instinctively covered her mouth to keep herself from making a noise. The troll laughed as he said, "Time's up bitch."

Willow's heart pounded quickly as she wondered what she could do. The troll had not seen her, so she could still sneak away. But she was still there, and she knew deep inside it had to do with a desire to help Luna, despite her feeling as if there was nothing she could do.

Just then she noticed a rock on the ground. Without a second thought, Willow grabbed the stone and threw it at the troll as hard as she could. When the rock hit the troll, he let go of Luna. Luna, who was surprisingly still conscious, noticed Willow. She shouted for Willow to run, but Willow couldn't move before the troll jumped in front of her.

He glared at Willow saying, "Looks like the second rat has finally arrived."

The troll grabbed the tree behind Willow and pulled it out of the ground. Willow watched in horror as he hoisted the tree over his head like a bat. He laughed as he said, "Bye, bye bitch."

He swung the tree at Willow, who quickly screamed, "NO!"

Instantly, blood-red fire shot out of Willow's hands, engulfing the troll and the tree he was holding. Willow had a fearful look on her face as she watched the troll who was screaming in pain burn to death. Suddenly Luna grabbed Willow's arm and yelled for her to run. Both women bolted as the burning troll and the tree he held fell to the ground.

They continued to run until Luna said, "I think we can stop. Oh, and my name is Luna, by the way."

Willow, who was panting, introduced herself. After a moment, Willow noticed Luna was holding the staff she had earlier, along with a blue purse.

As Luna searched through the purse, she said, "Thanks for your help. When I decided to hide out in this realm, I didn't expect to run into a troll. All the reports said there was no magic here."

"Wait, what?"

"I'm the princess of the planet Solspear, in realm F829L."

"I still don't get what you're saying."

"But you just used magic."

Willow looked at her hands for a moment before saying, "Fire just shot out of my hands. I, I saw fire shoot from my hands, but how did I do that?"

Luna said, "You used magic, unless, wait, did you not know you have magic powers? Wow, you pulled off a spell that powerful on your first try."

Luna pulled out a blue bottle and drank it. Instantly all her wounds healed. She then whispered something, and her staff disappeared, along with her wings.

Willow asked, "What just happened?"

"Let's talk about that somewhere else. The fire you started may have fizzled out, but it was too big of a blaze to go unnoticed."

Willow, who was still in shock, started to wonder how such a large fire just fizzled out. Luna suggested that they leave the park. They walked in silence until they reached the parking lot. To Willow's chagrin, she saw Sandy standing next to her bike. Sandy looked at Willow for a moment before exhaling.

Willow started to inquire about what Sandy was doing there. In a snarky tone, Sandy said, "Can't believe my dad was dumb enough to let you borrow his car. But you have always been the favorite child since he's dumbstruck by your crazy aunt. Anyway, I'm gone."

Sandy quickly jumped on her bike and sped off. Willow criticized herself for not giving Sandy a piece of her mind after what she said about Martha.

Luna said, "I'm confused."

Willow replied, “Don’t worry about her. She’s my aunt’s boyfriend’s daughter, and she loves being a bitch.”

“I get she has an attitude, but if she was worried, she should have just said so.”

“What are you talking about? She wasn’t worried.”

Luna explained, “When I noticed her, she looked like she was standing on pins and needles. When she saw you were with me, she exhaled like she’d been holding her breath for a while. So, she was worried.”

“How are you so sure about that?”

Luna answered, “Part of my tactical training was learning how to read people.” Changing the subject Luna said, “Can you take me to a pawnshop? I need to sell some jewels for some quick cash. At least, I think it’s called cash. Do you use cash in this realm?”

Willow answered, “Yes, and I have a lot of questions.”

“So do I, but I need to get some quick cash first.”

They both heard emergency sirens, so without a word, they jumped in the car.”

Chapter 5

Hotel Sleepover

It was dark outside as Willow drove closer to her neighborhood, with Luna in the passenger's seat. Willow was slowly calming down at the same time her mind wondered if what she had just seen and experienced in the park was real. The only thing that made it undeniable was the fact that Luna was sitting next to her in the passenger seat.

That wasn't the only thing causing her worry; her mind returned to her encounter with Sandy. She thought *Luna might have been right. Sandy may have been worried.*

As Willow pulled into her neighborhood, she immediately felt a strange mixture of joy and rage. She and Luna had come to a few decisions as soon as they got in the car. First, they were going to stop at Willow's house because, despite Willow's shock, she knew she was a dead woman if she kept Eric's car all night. Next, they agreed after Willow took Luna to the pawnshop, that they would head over to a hotel Luna booked. Willow would stay the night so they could talk about what happened.

When Willow parked on the street, she noticed all the lights in the house were off. Guessing that her aunt and uncle were asleep, she decided to write a note, informing them that she was staying at a friend's house so they wouldn't worry.

When they both got out of the car, Luna said, "So this is what houses look like here."

"Do houses look different where you are from?"

"Not dramatically different. It's just all buildings where I'm from are mostly made from red stone."

Willow said, "Interesting. Anyway, I want to get to the pawnshop quickly, but I want to put my aunt's boyfriend's car in the garage first. Well, that and I need to get the keys to my aunt's truck."

As both women walked towards the house, Luna asked, "Just you and your aunt live here?"

"Yes, for the most part. But my aunt's boyfriend and his children have been around practically my whole life."

"And you met them a little while after you and your aunt left that Texas place?"

"Yeah, Texas is a state."

"What do you mean by state?"

"I'll explain that at the hotel."

"Alright, your aunt seems to be unable to verbalize what she is trying to say when she tries to talk about when you lived in Texas."

Willow said, "Something like that."

"I have a few theories as to why that's happening, but I'll talk about that with you later."

Just then, Willow opened the door, and they walked into the house. When Willow turned on the light for the main area, someone turned the upstairs lights on. The two women soon realized it was Eric, when he walked downstairs. He turned on the light to the main area and then sighed in relief when he spotted Willow.

He said, "Thank goodness you're alright. I just heard there was some kind of fire in the park. Oh, I did not notice you were with a friend."

Willow said, "This is my friend Luna. We bumped into each other at the park. So, we decided to have a sleepover at her place."

"Ok, nice to meet you, Luna."

Luna replied, "Nice to meet you, sir."

Willow said, "I had no idea there was a fire in the park. But it does explain the emergency vehicles that Luna and I saw."

Eric said, "Yeah, the police are saying it was bizarre. People saw it shoot up out of nowhere then quickly disappear."

Luna said, "That's strange, but I'm glad Willow and I left before that happened." Eric said, "Me, too! Anyway, I'm going to bed, so you ladies have fun."

Before Eric headed up the stairs, Willow asked, "How is Aunt Martha doing?"

Eric answered, "She's better than she was. I think she will be fine if she gets some rest." After that, Eric went upstairs, and Willow went to grab her aunt's keys.

When she grabbed her keys, she realized she needed to pack some clothing. She turned on the TV and asked Luna to make herself comfortable for a few minutes. Willow bolted quickly upstairs to pack an overnight bag.

Willow's bedroom was a pretty unimpressive room. Willow and her aunt stayed at the Williams' home a lot, so most of Willow's things were in her room there. In the center of her room was her bed which was covered with a blue spread. The walls were baby blue, while the floors were the same gray hardwood as the rest of the house. The wall behind her bed had a window with the shade pulled down, and there was a closet on the right side of her room.

Willow saw her old bookbag lying in the corner of the room. Without a thought, she dumped everything in the bookbag onto the floor. She pulled out an outfit and PJs from her drawer. When Willow shoved the clothing into her book bag, she heard her aunt crying. Concerned, she quickly closed her bookbag and put it on before hurrying down the hall.

She reached her aunt's bedroom door. Willow barely touched the doorknob when she heard her aunt say, "She needs to know."

Curious, Willow pressed her ear against the door to hear better. She heard Eric say, "I agree. But how do we tell Willow everything? You can't even tell me the whole situation, so how can I explain it to her?"

Martha said, "Damn, this would be so much easier if my parents hadn't gotten involved. They ignored Willow and me for years. Now they just show up, and for their own selfish bullshit. I'm not letting them hurt her like they did me."

Using a reassuring tone, Eric said, "They won't succeed in getting Willow to do what they want."

Martha responded, "They pushed me into all three of my failed marriages."

Surprised, Eric asked, "You were married before? Is that why you won't marry me?"

"No, it's because my, my, m…."

Eric quickly said, "Martha, stop. I shouldn't have asked you that when you're not a hundred percent okay."

Martha said, "I'm sorry, Eric. There is so much you, Willow, and your children need to know."

"Don't apologize to me. This whole thing is not your fault."

Eric told Martha to get some sleep, and he was going to take a shower. Willow started to head downstairs as what she overheard weighed on her mind.

After going through the process of taking her aunt's car out of the garage, then putting Eric's car in the garage, she closed the garage and took off with Luna in her aunt's truck. Willow headed for a pawnshop that she found on her GPS, while Luna stared out the window.

As Willow meditated on what she heard, Luna, who was staring out the window, said, "It's funny. I was told everything in this realm would be very backwards, since this place supposedly didn't have magic. In the short time I've been here, this place is no way inferior to any other place I've been."

"How long have you been here?"

"Three days. Everything was fine until I bumped into that troll. That damn thing ate my suitcase."

"It ate your suitcase?"

"Sounds weird, yes, but that's what happened. I had checked out of my hotel because I wanted to go stay at this new hotel that just opened."

"Are you talking about the Celestial Hotel?"

"Yep, when I discovered this planet in this realm has the internet and cell phones like my world, I pawned some of my stuff and booked a hotel room. Later, when I found out about the nicer hotel, I reserved a room."

"Speaking of that, do you think we can get the room switched to two beds?"

"Yeah, I think so."

Willow commented, "I'm a little surprised you have technology where you're from. I figured everything was done with magic in Solspear."

Luna said, "We use magic for a lot of things. But science and technological innovations are a major thing where I'm from."

"So, how did you bump into that troll? My mind is still racing from that whole experience."

Luna began to explain, "After I booked the hotel, I decided to head to the park. I don't want to get into it, but I have some family stuff going on. The whole point of me even coming here was to take a little break from it before I start university."

"You're about to start college, too. Wow, that's ironic."

"Oh, I forgot you mentioned your upcoming college trip."

"Really, the college trip was a ruse to go to Texas to look for answers."

Luna inquired, "Answers about what?"

Willow thought, *stop talking about Texas, you don't know this weird fairy. But after what I saw, should I keep silent? My aunt's weirdness and my parents' disappearance may have something to do with magic. It doesn't matter if magic has anything to do with everything going on in my life, I need to be careful how much I share. I don't know this woman.*

Willow said, "I don't want to get into that."

"I understand. So, I'm still not sure why that troll attacked me, or why it ate my suitcase. To be honest, that thing eating my suitcase troubles me the most."

"Why?"

"Trolls strictly eat meat. So why would it choose to eat my suitcase? I didn't even use it to defend myself."

As Willow parked in the pawnshop's parking lot, she said, "Maybe it wanted to eat it so you would not consider using it as a weapon."

Luna said, "Maybe."

Luna got out of the car, saying she would be back in a moment. As soon as she was gone, Willow covered her mouth and screamed. Then she began hugging herself and breathing very hard. She felt her entire body trembling as she released heavy breaths. Willow did not know why the moment Luna left the car, she felt so overwhelmed. Her only real guess was she subconsciously had put on a brave face to protect herself because she did not fully trust Luna. Plus, she couldn't risk exposing the night's events while at home, considering the walls in her house are paper-thin. If she had let out that scream at home, even if she had muffled her voice with a pillow, her aunt or Eric would have heard her, and she would not have been able to pull herself together in time.

Willow started to calm herself down and as her breathing steadied, she questioned her logic in thinking she and Luna should share a room. Luna was a fairy from some kind of other dimension or whatever. It might not be the best idea to room with her. When that thought entered her mind, she did not feel completely better; however, the shaking stopped, letting her regain her composure.

Willow thought, *I never freaked out like that before. I never encountered a fairy being attacked by a troll until today, either. That was scary. No wonder magic caused Aunt Martha to have freak-outs. At least, I'm assuming that's what happened. My grandparents probably have magic, too. But if what I overheard was right, my grandparents may be a serious problem.*

She sat up in her seat while thinking, *is that why Aunt Martha doesn't want me to talk to them? How much does Uncle Eric know about this?* Willow exhaled. *Does Aunt Martha have magic powers, and is that the secret that you've been holding onto this whole time?*

Willow pulled out her phone and started to use some of her graduation money to book a room at the hotel. The second Luna got into the car, Willow told her that she had booked her own room. Luna smiled as she said, "I get to keep my king bed."

Willow said, "If you were looking forward to the room you picked, you could have just told me. Sorry, it's not about you. I was so focused on getting down to what happened earlier, that I didn't realize I wasn't really alright with us sharing a room. I was worried you would be insulted by me changing my mind."

Luna told Willow, "That's understandable. We don't know each other that well yet, and we have a lot to figure out."

Willow pulled up to the Celestial Hotel. The hotel was a large gray skyscraper, and the front of the hotel was lit up with different colored lights.

After Willow parked the car and as they got out, Luna said, "I have to go shopping."

"Oh right, a troll ate your suitcase. Can't you use some kind of spell to make an outfit?"

"I can, but it's not the type of stuff I need."

"What do you mean?"

"I'll explain it after we get settled in our rooms and order some drinks."

"Luna, how old are you?"

Luna answered, "Eighteen, why?"

"I'm the same age and we can't buy alcohol until we are twenty-one."

"I forgot this country's backward rules."

"It's not that backward of an idea."

"I may not have been here that long, but I did learn you can join the armed forces here when you turn eighteen."

"So?"

"Come on, Willow, you can sign up to risk your life at eighteen, but you can't have a drink because it's more dangerous than a war zone."

Thoughtfully, Willow said, "I see your point. But I'm not about to try to be sneaky to buy beer, and I'm not really in the mood to drive home just to get booze."

Luna inquired, "Your aunt lets you drink?"

"I turned eighteen a couple of weeks ago, and my aunt told me that since I'm a legal adult and as long as I was responsible and only drank in the house, then she doesn't care if I touch her alcohol. I just can't tell my Uncle Eric what she said. He's more sensitive about me drinking."

"Oh."

"She may have permitted me to touch her alcohol, but I don't fix myself a drink that often because when I was fourteen, I got super drunk at a party."

Smiling, Luna said, "Seriously?"

Willow began to tell her story, "Yep, my crazy ass thought I could handle booze. When a group of the other teens at the party pulled out a drink called purple haze, I decided to impress everyone by proving I could drink a large glass of it. The truth was that I had never had a drink in my life before that night."

"Oh shit, how drunk did you get?"

Willow continued, "I passed out. To this day, I am so glad two of my friends were there. They got me out of that party and took me home. When I woke up, I spent the rest of the night throwing up in the toilet. I spent the next morning being yelled at by my aunt and Uncle Eric while my head was pounding in pain as a result of my first hangover."

As soon as the word hangover escaped her lips, Willow recalled every minute of the night she got drunk. Willow was lying on her side with a bucket next to her bed in case she needed to throw up. Sandy came into her room and called her a lightweight. Willow begged Sandy to leave, but instead, Sandy forced Willow to sit up.

She handed Willow a glass of a nasty-looking brown liquid. Sandy bugged Willow until she drank the nasty potion. Willow cringed while thinking about how bad the liquid tasted. But it did ease Willow's hangover.

Her thoughts were interrupted by Luna asking, "Are you ok?"

"Yeah, I was just remembering my first hangover."

Luna said, "If we can't have booze, then how about a chocolate sundae?"

Willow thought, *I didn't get any pie.* She said, "That sounds like a good idea. We don't need to deal with any more drama tonight."

Luna, in a whispered tone, revealed to Willow, "Speaking of drama. Don't freak out, but I'm not supposed to be here."

Surprised, Willow said, "What, why?"

"I was going to tell you this when I was explaining the realms."

"You know what? Get ice-cream and some coffee."

Luna inquired, "Why do we need coffee?"

"It's going to be a long night. We're going to need something to keep us awake."

Chapter 6

Realms and Magic

After checking in and putting her things away, Willow headed to Luna's room. The hallway floors of the hotel were covered with a dark blue carpet dotted with tiny white stars. The walls were white, and each door was painted the same blue color as the carpet, with each individual room identified with gold numbers. There were several black and gold sconces spread intermittently along the hallway walls, giving the hallway a warm ambience. Willow did not wish to think about anything as she walked. All the insanity of fairies, trolls and magic was too much for her. But her mind decided to reflect on Sandy giving her that drink for her hangover all those years ago. She vaguely remembered Sandy saying not to tell anyone she brought her something for her hangover.

Willow started to wonder why Sandy said that. As Willow pondered more about Sandy's behavior that day, she remembered what her aunt said to her when she recovered. She had gone downstairs to eat a little bread since she was hungry, but her stomach was still upset. The moment she set foot downstairs, she bumped into her aunt.

Martha snapped, "I hope your little ass learned your lesson. If you haven't, don't worry, you're grounded for three months. So, you have plenty of time to think about what you did."

"I know, and I promise I will never get drunk again."

"You sure as hell better keep your word about that. I'm surprised you're up and about."

"Well, that gross stuff you had Sandy send up really worked."

Surprise in her tone, Martha said, "Sandy was here?"

"Yeah, she brought me some nasty brown stuff."

"That child has had way too many hangovers. I guess she heard about what you did and took pity on you."

Willow asked, "Why would she make me something for my hangover? Then make fun of me because I got drunk?"

"Sandy is complicated."

Willow snapped, "Or just a jerk."

As Willow thought about what her aunt said, she reflected on what Sandy had done earlier. Sandy had been cruel to her for so long. Did this attitude blind Willow to when Sandy was trying to be nice? Or was she just deluding herself because she missed the person Sandy used to be?

When she reached Luna's room, she took a breath before she knocked on the door. Luna opened the door, greeted Willow, and welcomed her inside. The second Willow set foot in Luna's room her jaw dropped.

Luna's room had a fancy dining area, with a glass dining table and gray dining chairs. There was a crystal chandelier hanging above the table, and a glass vase with blueish purple irises in the center of the table. Opposite the dining area to the right side of the room was a lounge area. There was a gray carpet underneath a glass coffee table. To the left and right of the coffee table were white armchairs. Behind the coffee table was a white couch that had blue pillows sitting on each end. The front wall was a massive window with a fantastic view of the city. The left wall had a door in the center leading to Luna's bedroom.

As Willow and Luna sat at the table, Willow noticed two oval shaped glass bowls filled with French vanilla bean ice-cream, which had been covered with chocolate and caramel syrup. Both girls dug into the ice cream. Even as the sweet taste of the ice cream danced across her tongue, Willow could not take her mind off her troubles.

Luna took a breath before saying, "Ok, I guess I must go first since I'm the one who knows more about the realms and magic. Are you aware of the multi-verse?"

Willow responded, "I know a little about the multi-verse theory. It's supposed to be a theory where there are infinite planes of reality."

Luna said, "I guess people here think it's a theory. The multi-verse is real, and each plane of reality is known as a realm. I think it was over one hundred thousand years ago when a planet called Conzol in realm D000 became the supposed first place to discover how to travel to different realms."

"What do you mean by supposed first place?"

Luna continued, "Because there are infinite realms, it's hard to know the true first place that travelled between realms. Conzol, as far as scholars can tell, was the first place that figured out how to travel to different realms. As they learned more about the realms, they found some absolute truths about them. First, there is an infinite version of yourself, where you're from, people you know, and your planet. When it comes to the versions of yourself, sometimes, they are exactly the same as you. Other times they are different in the sense of their personality or their species. There are even infinite realms where a version of you does not exist."

"Hold up. There are really different species of me?"

"I know. That's so weird."

Willow, as she ate her ice cream, was surprised that as it hit her stomach, it only helped Willow relax a tiny bit. Usually junk food brightens her spirits.

However, Luna noticing Willow was still in distress, said, "Why don't I order some margaritas?"

"I told you we are too young to buy alcohol."

"I know, but I was so worried about everything that happened that I forgot that my fake ID says I'm twenty-two."

Willow said, "I don't know why I was surprised for a moment when you mentioned a fake ID. I feel like I actually do need a drink, so bring on the margaritas."

Luna picked up the phone and called room service. When she got off the phone, she looked at Willow and said, "The man on the phone said they will have someone bring us a couple of mango margaritas soon."

Wanting to get to the heart of the matter, Willow said, "Ok, so there are all these different planes of existence where I may or may not bump into a version of myself."

Luna, offering more information, continued, "Yes. So, to make travel between realms easier, an interdimensional council and registry was formed. All known realms are registered by the council in order to regulate travel between them. For example, I am from planet Solspear in realm F829, and right now, we are on Earth in realm C157. In addition to keeping a record of which known realm is which, the council makes sure people don't travel to other realms where another version of themselves exists. They even manage trade and political affairs between realms, so that things don't get out of hand."

"Ok, I think I understand."

"Good, so the reason why the council makes sure to keep all political affairs calm is because of the multiverse war."

"Let me make sure I know what you mean by that. So, since there are infinite realms, the council labels all the realms they are aware of."

"Yep." For nearly thirty minutes Luna continued to explain the details of life in the multiverse.

Willow interrupted, "Ok, so when this multiverse war broke out, you're referring to a few realms going to war- not every realm in existence?"

"Exactly. I think about ten realms were involved in the war. When these realms went to war, it caused them to explode, creating a new distorted realm known as realm LV345."

"Where are those margaritas? This is making my head hurt."

Luna laughed, "I understand. It bothered me, too when my tutor explained it."

"Ok, so I am going to try not to think too hard about this whole war between dimensions because then I'm going to start thinking about other factors that will make my head hurt. Before we get more into realm LV345, why were those other realms at war?"

Luna answered, "I'm not going to get into why the realms were fighting because the reasons for the war and who was fighting for what gets complicated. I would need a couple of months with charts just to explain it all, and we have to go to Texas soon."

"You're coming to Texas with me?"

Luna offered, "I would like to if you don't mind me tagging along. Knowing you have magic and your aunt's strange behavior; I have a bad feeling something dangerous might happen."

Willow gratefully accepted, "I would love to have you come with us. The more I think about my aunt, the more I have a feeling magic is involved."

Luna assured, "Magic is involved."

"What?"

Luna said, "I promise to explain, but please let me explain the realms first. Because if I don't, then you won't fully grasp what I have to say about your aunt."

"As long as you tell me what's wrong with her after you explain this realms mess."

Luna finished the last of her ice cream and said, "I will, I promise. So, realm LV345 is a bizarre place that's full of monsters and crazy people."

Willow questioned, "Crazy how?"

"They want to destroy other realms in the name of chaos. There are other realms with monsters, but the majority of the ones that are known don't have aggressive monsters. The troll that attacked me earlier was from planet Vasferd in realm X40789. As far as anyone in the current known realms is aware of, all trolls come from there. Since realm LV345 and the troll world cause so much trouble, three realms found a way to prevent the problems from getting too out of hand.

Sadly, the realms that deal with the problem are overwhelmed trying to keep it under control. At least, I think they are. They constantly send soldiers from several galaxies within their realm to fight the creatures from realm LV345. They are doing this without any aid from the other realms aligned with the council. The council itself discourages other realms from even getting involved with or helping the three realms who are fighting against realm LV345."

Willow commented, "That seems all kinds of sketchy. What are they doing about that troll place in X40789."

"They try to monitor it and prevent trolls from leaving. So, do you have any questions about the different realms?"

Willow asked, "Yes, so how many known realms have magic?"

Luna answered, "I'm not sure. Realms that have magic are not supposed to travel to non-magic realms. Like many royals, the rules don't really apply to me as long as I don't get caught."

"What happens if you get caught?"

"In my case, I have to issue an apology to the council while the incident is played off as a prank. An everyday person would be looking at twenty years in the council's prison. They don't care if it was an accident. In other words, let's keep that whole thing with you accidentally casting a fire spell between us. You don't deserve to be punished for a situation that's not your fault."

"Thanks for the warning. Is it possible for the council to find out what I did?"

"No, and if they find out about the fire, I'll just say I did it to protect myself from the troll. The political hailstorm that will erupt will make the council want to brush it under the rug. But there is no point in talking about it. This place is one of the few realms the council doesn't keep a close watch on, which is one of the reasons why I came to stay here for a little while. It will also make it easier to teach you magic."

Willow smiled as she said, "You're really going to teach me spells?"

Luna assured her, "Yeah, if I don't, you might unintentionally get yourself into a lot of trouble. Speaking of trouble, I think I know what's wrong with your aunt. I sensed a pretty powerful curse coming from upstairs when I was at your house. When your aunt's boyfriend came downstairs, I didn't sense any curse on him. So, I think all this mess with your aunt is really a curse."

Willow took a breath before saying, "I'm not surprised. Early this morning, I thought my aunt had a form of PTSD. Sometime after the whole park incident, I realized magic might be responsible. I'm wondering if I'm even from here."

"You're probably not."

Willow felt herself tremble while she said, "How do I even find out where I'm from? Am I even a human?"

Luna hugged Willow for a moment before saying, "It's ok, Willow. You're definitely a human."

Willow forced herself to hold back tears as she asked, "How do you know?"

Luna, in a reassuring tone, said, "Outside of the fact that you look human, when someone uses magic, a magical signature is left behind. It only lasts a few minutes, but when I sensed yours, I could tell it was human. The real problem is finding out whether you're a fairy, witch, dragon, druid, genie, etcetera. You may even be more than one."

"I don't understand what you mean by that. Aren't all those creatures not human?"

Luna said, "Willow, I don't know what people define fairies as in this realm, but in all the known realms all fairies are one hundred percent human. Turning into a dragon, phoenix or sprouting fairy wings is a transformative state that happens when large amounts of magic power are needed."

Willow asked, "Do witches have a transformative state?"

"They are the only ones who don't. They're also the only ones who can fly without practicing."

"I think I get it now, but how do we figure out which magic being I am?"

"We have to discover your magic type. Being a witch, fairy or any other magic user means you wield a particular type of magic. I'll run a test on you later to figure out which type of magic wielder you are. Right now, we should talk about the uncomfortable stuff."

"You mean my aunt being under a curse?"

Luna said, "Yep."

"Shit, am I under a curse?"

"No, I don't sense one on you."

"Great, but do you think my aunt knows she's cursed?"

"Most definitely, and from what you told me about her I would not be surprised if she wants to tell you about it. The problem is she can't because she's well, you know, cursed."

"I should just confront her about all this."

"Bad idea. We don't know squat about the curse she's under. Confronting her about it might cause her mind to break."

"Crap, then what should we do?"

"What you were already planning to do in the first place. But when we get to wherever this Texas place is, we need to make sure your friends and Vanessa don't follow us to your old house. Also, we need to prepare to run if things get bad."

Willow thought, *she's right. We've got to be careful. Should I mention my grandparents? Luna is talking about a potential threat. If I talk to her about them, it might shed some light on what we have to worry about when we get to Texas.*

Willow took a breath before saying, "There is something else I need to tell you."

"Ok."

"Earlier, my aunt told me a little bit about my grandparents. Her boyfriend thinks my grandparents are trying to contact me, and my aunt doesn't want me to talk to them."

Luna frowned as she said, "Keep avoiding them for now."

"Are you sure?"

"If your grandparents are trying to contact you now, there is a very real chance they could have done that a long time ago. Interdimensional calling is not hard, and they didn't try to talk to you. Also, it's a one-way call to presumed non-magic realms."

"What does that mean?"

"They can call you, but you can't call them. There is a chance your grandparents may be trying to use you."

"What could they use me for?"

"From what you said about the man you suspect is your dad, I think your grandparents are nobles or social climbers, which means your mom may have been subjected to a magic merging marriage."

"That sounds bad."

With sadness in her voice, Luna said, "It is, and a lot of people get hurt- especially babies. In magic matching, a man and woman are wed in hopes of creating a child with strong magical powers, or in hopes the baby will inherit a certain type of rare magic. You can't tell what kind of magic a child has until it's close to time for the mom to give birth.

This is not pleasant, but I think telling you this is the only way to provide you with a full idea of how terrible it is. My parents were forced into a magical match marriage, and they were grateful for my little brother and me. They both longed for the opportunity to experience the joy of having children. The agreement with their marriage was to have two children that had powerful magic and inherited my family's power to summon a sun staff. They had one baby boy before me who did not have strong magic. So, my grandfather had my brother kill him right after he was born."

Shocked, Willow said, "I'm so sorry that's just horrible!"

"I think going through that messed up my folks. My dad is in constant fear that something horrible is going to happen to me or my little brother. My mom spends most of her time at my deceased brother's grave crying. Also, they both drink a lot. One time my dad got so drunk he tried to kill his mistress with an ax."

"I thought your dad was a king."

"He is, and that's why no one tried to punish him for it. But he's too lost in his own world of alcohol and women. He's pretty much left my uncle in charge of the kingdom. It's also why my brother and I were raised by my cousin Markel and his wife Yolanda. But if I'm right, then you probably inherited some kind of special power. Your mother's husband probably did not want a girl to have it, so he wanted you gone."

Willow said, "This is too much."

"I agree."

The two girls were silent for a few minutes when there was a knock on the door. Luna answered it, and it soon became clear it was the margarita delivery. After getting the drinks, Luna gave Willow one of the margaritas. Luna took two big gulps out of hers and placed her drink on the table. Willow, on the other hand, only took a few small sips out of hers before putting it down. She wanted to drink more but reminded herself she would finish it too quickly. Willow did not want to develop a habit of stress drinking, so she told herself to nurse her margarita.

Willow said, "So if I inherited some kind of special magic, then my grandparents may be trying to contact me to marry me off."

"Maybe, but right now there is no way for us to know. I guess the next order of business we have to handle is my encounter with that troll. Its presence means beings from Vasferd X40789 and realm LV345 are getting past the three realms who are supposed to keep them from escaping. I can't contact my cousin or his wife about this because I'm in this realm. But that would not be an option even if I could. If my uncle hears about this, he'll try to get permission to send a team to purge this planet of all magic, which is to basically kill all life on this planet."

Willow asked, "What? Why would he do that?"

"If magic starts to show up in a realm where the council thought it did not exist, then it might be a sign of magic migration. The council and many aristocrats do not like that. So, they opt to kill everything there if they assume that's what is going on."

"Luna, I don't like any of this. The council is full of jackasses who want to control every realm they find."

"It's what they do. Shit, I almost forgot I need to get you a fake ID."

"I'm guessing for interdimensional travel?"

"Yeah, but first let's figure out what kind of magic wielder you are."

"How do we do that?"

Luna finished her drink before saying, "Stand up."

As Willow stood up, Luna quickly drank the remainder of her ice cream. After saying she should get some water because of how sweet the ice cream was, Luna stood up then snapped her fingers, and the rod she had been holding earlier appeared in her right hand. She gripped the rod with both hands as she backed up a little bit before pointing it at Willow.

Luna said, "A lot of lights are going to swirl around you. Don't touch them. Keep your eyes open and stand as still as possible."

Willow felt nervous as her body tensed up. She stood as stiff as a board. Meanwhile, Luna looked Willow in the eyes as she said, "licaro melosta."

Suddenly green and pink orbs of light shot out of the end of Luna's staff. The lights quickly swirled around Willow. The whirling of the lights caused Willow to feel dizzy, but trying as hard as she could to follow Luna's instructions, Willow forced herself to keep her eyes open and stand still. Thankfully the lights suddenly stopped and remained halted in midair. In an instant some of the lights turned black. Other lights turned red, and the remainder turned blue. Then one by one they began to disappear.

Once the lights were gone, Luna said, "Darn it. Oh, sorry Willow, you can move now."

In a shaky voice, Willow asked, "Is something wrong?"

"Not really. Your powers fit multiple types of magic users, and I only know what one of them is."

Willow nervously asked, "So, a person can be more than one type of magic user?"

"Yep, but it's not a common trait. That's why I barely mentioned it."

"Oh, that's right you did say something about being more than one magic type."

Luna explained, "The lights turned three different colors and some of them turned different sizes. The black ones got a little bigger, the blue ones got smaller, and the red ones remained the same size. I don't know what the blue or black lights mean because of their sizes, but I will look it up sometime tomorrow. But the good news is you are a fairy like me, which means you can get gifts from designers with me in the morning."

Willow felt her whole world stop as she said, "I'm a fairy. Wow, I am actually a fairy."

"And we are getting gifts from designers in the morning."

Willow questioned, "Oh right, wait, why are we getting gifts from designers?"

"I'm a princess, so designers make money when I'm seen wearing their items- clothing, jewelry etc. As my friend you would get free stuff because you would be seen with me. Also, you are going to have the extra perk of being one of Duke Monticello's kids. Well, at least people will think you are, after I get your ID made."

"Won't someone get suspicious about that? He must know his own children?"

Luna laughed and said, "The man has fifty-six kids and new ones are popping up every day. He's also an active voice for the anti-condoms movement and demands that all women get their tubes tied."

"He sounds like a jackass."

"Get this, he's in paternity court all the time trying to get out of paying child support. Practically every paternity judge in several of the known realms do not even want to preside over any of his cases because he thinks telling a judge he was minding his own business will somehow mean he's not the father."

"Is there any way we can see one of these cases?"

"Yeah, I have interdimensional app streaming."

"Cool, but won't somebody check?"

"No."
"Ok, if you say so."
Luna announced, "Alright, I guess we should get some sleep."

Chapter 7

Let's Go Shopping!!!

Willow's hotel room, although not as impressive as Luna's, was very nice. Her bed was near the back wall while a tv sat on a metal tv stand painted gold near the front wall. A door leading to the bathroom was on the back left wall a few feet away from her bed, while a window covered by a large white curtain was on the right wall.

Willow lay in her bed staring at the celling. Her Uncle had called her just a few hours earlier. Thankfully, her aunt was feeling better, but he decided he wanted to have her move in with him by the end of the week. Apparently, he got her aunt to agree with him. So, Willow needed to decide what she wanted to take to the Williams estate, and what she wanted to sell.

She rolled over onto her side while she thought, *Dammit. I don't want to live with Sandy. I'm almost eighteen. Maybe they'll let me stay at the house until it's time for college. Uncle Eric sounded very eager about us moving in. He's probably crazy about the idea of us finally all living in the same house. Can't blame him for feeling like that, especially since once the school year starts, I'm moving on campus.*

Just then Willow remembered what her aunt said about being married before. Then her mind started to wonder what kind of men her aunt married. Were her marriages magic match marriages like the one Lunas parents were subjected to? Or were the reasons completely different? The more she thought about it the more her head hurt. Willow sat up and decided she might as well get out of bed and shower. As she climbed out of bed her phone rang. Looking at the screen she realized that it was her aunt and she answered.

She heard Martha say, "Willow how are you?"

"I'm good, Auntie. Glad you're feeling better. Uncle Eric told me to start preparing for us to move full-time to his place."

"Yeah, he got me to push the move up by promising me he won't try to get me to sell the house."

"Why do you want to keep the house?"

"Well, you know I've made it my mission to update the living room. More importantly, the house is in a prime location."

"Oh, so it's too soon to sell it."

"I guess you could say that. Anyway, do you still have that toy lock picking set?"

"No, remember it broke."

"I don't remember it breaking."

"Remember Sandy and I broke it when we were pretending to break into the cookie jar? Why do you need it anyway?"

"No reason. A customer and I were talking about an art thief recently, and for some reason I remembered how you three girls liked to pretend to be cat burglars when you were little. So, I got curious about the lock picking set."

"Oh, ok."

Martha continued, "Anyway, kiddo, I'm heading over to your Uncle Thomas's new restaurant. Some pieces of art I ordered are supposed to arrive today. So, I need to inspect them before the order is accepted."

"Ok, Auntie, I will talk to you later."

"Oh, Willow, I almost forgot. Eric told me about your friend Luna. Why don't you bring her to dinner tonight? Eric's chef is making steaks."

Willow replied, "Ok, I'll ask her."

After Willow hung up, she took a deep breath. When she exhaled, she told herself to get a shower then go and see Luna.

Willow, while sitting on Luna's couch, took note of the fact that Luna had a frustrated look on her face and seemed to be scrolling feverously on her tablet. Out of concern that something was amiss, Willow asked if everything was alright.

Luna said, "I'm fine. Some of the stylists I wanted us to get clothes from are being a pain."

Willow, who was looking forward to the new outfits, asked, "How?"

Luna replied, "They are trying to get me to get clothes from them on specific dates, which means it's a setup for a media event. I'm not interested in any media fair when I'm trying to give myself a break before I go to university."

"Where are you going to college?"

"Almerea, it's a university that specializes in training politicians, fighters, and magic scholars."

"Oh, I wish I could make up my mind about which school I want to go to."

"You do need to gain a grasp on magic. Maybe you should consider Almerea."

"I don't know if I can even get in, or what to say to my aunt and her boyfriend about it."

"If you want to go, I can write a letter of recommendation. They will let you in without question, and they won't even check your credentials."

"I'm a little concerned about that."

"Don't worry. I can only get away with that because Almerea is on Solspear."

"Ok, I'll think about it."

"Ok."

"So, are you going to start teaching me magic?"

"Let's do that later. You're going to need a lot of outfits if you don't want to end up naked every time you cast a spell."

"Why does that happen?"

"Magic generates an energy strong enough to rip normal fabric easily. In the past, spell-casters would use transformation spells to clothe themselves before using magic. My cousin Yolanda said it was embarrassing because a person would be naked for a few seconds before a weird light surrounded them, followed by weird fabrics wrapping around you making a new outfit. Unfortunately, the outfit would look like something from a comic."

"That sounds embarrassing."

Luna announced, "Luckily magic proof clothing was gaining popularity when she was fourteen, so she thankfully didn't have to deal with that for long. Ok, found someone who will give me clothes now. After we're done, I will teach a spell."

"I'm kind of excited about transforming into a fairy."

"It's not really what we would consider transforming. You have all your powers whether your wings are out or not. The wings are something that appear when you summon them or you're using a great deal of magic power."

"Wow."

"Alright, let's pick up some outfits."

Luna pressed an app on her tablet. Suddenly a doorway to a clothing shop appeared next to the coffee table. Willow's heart jumped the moment the doorway appeared.

Wow! Willow thought to herself, *will I ever be able to adjust to magic?*

Luna said, "Oh crap, I almost forgot."

She then snapped her fingers, and a strange glowing light flashed, and a blue card appeared. It hovered in midair in front of Willow. Willow felt uncomfortable with the idea of touching the card. Luna said, "I know the card looks strange, but it's safe go ahead and grab it."

Willow asked, "What is it?"

"It's the identification card I told you that you'll need for interdimensional travel."

"Oh, umm ok."

Willow slowly reached for the ID card. When she finally grabbed it, she took a close look at it. There was no photo on the ID; however, it did read "Duchess Willow Monticello". *Never thought I would be using a fake ID for interdimensional travel.*

Willow followed Luna through the doorway. The inside of the clothing shop had gray walls and light brown wood floors. In the center of the room was a round couch with white fabric. There was a front desk near the right side of the room with two white doors behind it. Luna sat down on the couch, and Willow looked around the room.

Willow, adjusting to the idea of a designer shop, smiled. She would normally shop online for clothes because there were more options from the stores she likes.

Two minutes passed when a woman with pointy ears, wearing the strangest outfit Willow had ever seen, entered the room. The woman had brown skin and orange eyes, with gold glitter eyeshadow decorating her eyelids. Her hair was pink like cotton candy and was even shaped like cotton candy.

The woman's outfit looked like it was a purple plum costume with a dinosaur tail attached to the bottom. Willow thought, *keep your composure. This elf lady would probably be weirded out if I looked shocked that elves exist. At the same time, though, what the hell is she wearing? I hope Luna is not planning to make me wear that high fashion crap.*

The woman curtsied before saying, "Your highness, it is an honor to be in your presence. I have prepared the clothes you requested. If there are any problems, please don't hesitate to make me aware."

Luna replied, "Thank you, Janet."

Janet smiled before clapping her hands once. Suddenly a long rack filled with clothes appeared out of nowhere. Willow's heart began to race when the clothing racks appeared. She started to approach it when Janet snapped, "Those are for her highness. You are too low in status to even touch them."

Luna groaned as she said, "That's enough, Janet. Willow is my friend and has every right to look at the clothing if she pleases."

Janet's attitude changed instantly. Quickly she said,"Oh, please forgive me, Miss Willow."

Not wishing to interact with Janet more than she needed to, Willow said, "It's fine."

Willow began looking through the clothes. After finding a few pieces she liked, she took them off the rack. She decided to hold onto them instead of trying them on in the changing room. Janet's attitude bothered Willow. Sure, Luna straightened Janet out, but Janet was clearly someone who was stuck-up. Eric had taught Willow to never associate with people like that.

Once she was sure she had everything she liked from the clothing rack, Willow asked Luna if she wanted to take a look at the clothes. Luna replied, "No, I'm just going to take the rest of the clothes with me and decide what I want."

Luna started to stand up when Janet said, "Your highness, wait, your wig is looking a little worn. Why not allow me to give you a better one?"

Immediately Luna shot Janet with a look like she was going to kill her. In a stern tone she said, "Janet, you never offered Willow a bag for her clothes. Do you expect her to carry them around like a vagabond?"

Willow tried not to laugh at hearing Luna use the word vagabond. Meanwhile, Janet conjured up a red bag that read "Ziggy's". She then rushed over to take the clothes from Willow. Janet snapped her fingers twice, and all the clothes folded before floating into the bag. After Janet handed the bag to Willow, Luna snapped her fingers, and all the clothes on the rack disappeared. As Willow and Luna headed back through the portal, Janet wished them a good day and to come back soon. Willow told Janet to have a good day, but Luna would not even acknowledge her.

When Willow and Luna were both back in Luna's room, Luna waved her hand and the portal closed. Willow noticed that all the clothes Luna had made disappear were sitting on the dining table, folded. Luna plopped herself down on the couch as she exhaled. When Willow sat down next to her Luna said, "I'm sorry."

As Willow sat her bag of clothes down next to her she replied, "You don't need to apologize to me for anything."

"It's just I didn't want your first experience going into another dimension to be a bad one."

"Luna, it's fine. Sure, that Janet person is a rude kiss ass, but I still got a lot of nice clothes, and I learned that elves are real."

"Elves are real, but Janet isn't an elf."

Willow, surprised, said, "Really?"

"She's a hobgoblin who went through plastic surgery so that she could work for a fashion designer named Ziggy because she wanted to move up into high society."

"What is a hobgoblin?"

Luna explained, "They are imps who have a habit of always being up to something nefarious. Some are born with very twisted noses that look like a corkscrew. Hobgoblins born that way tend to be extremely talented magic wielders. Ziggy hates hobgoblins because a hobgoblin burned down her family's house when she was a child. Janet thought if she made her nose look human, then Ziggy wouldn't notice she was a hobgoblin.

Unfortunately for Janet, Ziggy did notice. Ziggy only hired Janet to keep her as a sales associate and never allowed her to move up in social status, which pissed Janet off, but she can't quit for fear that Ziggy will make sure that she can't get another job. Janet can't even get any help from her family or other hobgoblins because in their community if you have a twisted nose and get rid of it, then you have insulted the hobgoblin race as a whole. It's an unforgivable action."

"Wow, so she has that attitude because things did not go her way?"

Luna corrected Willow. "No, she has that attitude because she's a spoiled bitch. Even before she got surgery on her nose, I heard she had a horrible attitude."

Willow inquired, "Are you sure you should trust a rumor?"

"I agree it's stupid to follow a rumor on blind faith; however, I learned the rumors were true when I met her parents at an event. Anyway, enough about her. We need to talk about basic spells."

"Yeah, you're right. My aunt is expecting us for dinner, so we only have so much time."

"Ok, it's going to be a while before you can summon your wings whenever you want, but when you do, you're going to want to be wearing pants."

"Why do I.... it's to make sure no one looks up my skirt, isn't it?"

"Yes, anyway, let's start practicing with a hair changing spell. Afterwords, I will help you with wing summoning. It will be a while before you succeed, but if you start working on it now you will probably get the hang of it in a month."

"Ok, but why are we starting with a hair spell?"

"If you mess it up, I can fix it easily."

Luna then surprised Willow by removing her wig, revealing that her hair was gray. After putting her wig on the table, Luna said, "I guess I need to explain spell types."

"Didn't we do that when you did that thing that showed us that I'm a fairy?"

"That was to identify what kind of magic user you are, not spell types. There are thirteen spell types, and it would take hours to explain each one. There are also differences between light and dark magic. We are going to focus on light and dark magic because I have to tell you what those are. Where do I begin? This is kind of complicated, too, so I'll give you a basic idea of what the differences are. Light magic is for defensive spells, and dark magic is for attacking. This does not mean you can't use dark magic for defense, or light magic for attacking. However, the number of light and dark magic spells that do this is small. That's why it's better to mostly rely on light magic for defense and dark magic for attacking.

There are other things that both dark and light magic are used for. I'll explain that later, partially because we don't have time. I feel we may run into trouble, and I don't want you to be defenseless. Ok, the spell I'm going to teach you has nothing to do with fighting. It's a simple light magic spell that will help you get used to magic. It's also super weak, so you don't have to worry about it burning your clothes off."

"I almost forgot about the clothing thing."

"Word of advice, you should just not wear any of your old clothes after today."

"I think you're right. I don't want to accidently end up naked in public if I cast a simple spell."

"Let's start the hair spell. As you can see, my hair is white. This is because of family magic."

"Are you talking about the hereditary magic?"

Luna continued, "Yes, and it turned my hair from brown to gray when I was five. Unfortunately, it prevents the hair changing spell from lasting on me for long. But you will be able to get the idea of the spell. Let's get into light magic. So, this spell is a light magic spell. Most light magic spells do not use as much magic power as dark magic."

Willow said thoughtfully, "Interesting."

Luna said, "Let's begin. For this spell you need to place both hands on your head and close your eyes. Then picture what you want your hair to look like. I'll do the spell first to give you a better idea of what to do."

Luna closed her eyes and put her hands on her head. Suddenly, Luna's hair changed from gray to brown and curly. She looked at Willow and said, "See? It's easy."

"Um, I guess so."

Luna's hair quickly began to change back to its original gray color. She said, "I get you're a little scared about casting your first spell, but trust me, you'll get the hang of it quickly."

Willow, unsure, responded, "Alright, if you say so."

Willow closed her eyes and put her hands on her head. She then envisioned having an afro. After a second, she heard Luna say, "Oh my, don't worry I can fix this. Willow opened her eyes and looked at Luna and in a concerned voice asked, "What happened?"

Luna waved her hand and a hand mirror suddenly appeared. Willow looked in the mirror only for the image reflected to make her jump out of her skin. Her hair had been straightened and covered in large yellow spots. Luna patted Willow's hair once, causing her hair to revert to its original style.

Willow said, "I'm glad I was able to use magic, but I was hoping to get the spell on the first try."

"Don't worry about it. You never used magic on purpose before, so it takes a little while for you to get the hang of it. Now that I think about it, was there anything else you were thinking about when you tried the spell?"

"The whole troll incident was in the back of my head."

"Hmmm, I'm not surprised. Sometimes a troublesome thought can interfere with a spell. It's normal for a person to have all sorts of random thoughts enter their minds when they're trying to concentrate. It looks like we need to work on your ability to suppress troublesome thoughts."

Willow questioned, "I can't have a troublesome thought at all? She thought to herself, *my mind is so filled with negative thoughts. How am I ever going to be able to cast spells*?"

Luna said, "You can't one hundred percent keep yourself from having negative thoughts, but you can suppress the thoughts enough to prevent them from interfering with your thought process when casting a spell."

"Ok, so what do I need to do?"

Luna explained, "Meditation will help you learn to control your thoughts."

Willow commented in disbelief, "Seriously?"

Luna, surprised by Willows reaction, said, "What? meditation helps calm the mind."

"Sorry, I guess I was hoping there would be some kind of magical quick fix for this."

Luna laughed as she said, "Trust me, you do not want anyone using magic on your brain if you can help it."

Using her phone, Luna began streaming a calming ambient noise. Luna instructed Willow to just focus on the peaceful sounds and try to think of nothing but the sound.

Willow sat on the floor trying to meditate, but her mind sadly seemed to refuse to stop thinking about her troubles. After thirty minutes Willow slammed her fist on the floor as she said, "Dammit. I give up I just can't do this."

Luna replied "Calm down. I believe you can learn to meditate. We're just approaching it the wrong way. When I began learning meditation, I was young and had never experienced anything traumatic. You, on the other hand, have been dealing with family issues, and the stress that results from that can be overwhelming. On top of that, the events of yesterday must have been mind blowing. Seeing a troll and a fairy for the first time, well, maybe not a fairy, since every time you look in a mirror you see a fairy- still, you had no idea who you are and that you have magic."

"Meaning, I can't meditate, so I can't learn magic."

"Calm down, Willow, you can learn magic. I'm just saying that the stress you've been under is getting in the way. We probably should wait a couple of days before having you attempt meditation or casting any spells. Give yourself time to get used to the idea."

Willow took a breath before saying, "Fine, I guess you're right. What time is it?"

"Two Thirty."

"Crap, I better go start packing. We need to be at my uncle's house by three o'clock."

"Ok, but change into one of your new outfits while you pack up."

"Why?"

"Your new clothes are infused with magic. It will probably feel a little funny wearing it for a while just because you're not used to it."

"Whoa wait, I have to adjust to my clothes making me feel tingly or something?"

"It feels more like occasionally being poked by a push pin."

Willow replied, "Really sounds odd."

"Yeah, but it only last five minutes, and it's only going to happen the first three times you wear them."

"Why?"

"Your magic and the magic in the clothing have to adjust to one another."

"I will feel a pricking sensation every time I put on a new magic outfit?"

Luna answered, "No, just the first three times you wear a magic outfit in general. After that you will never feel magic clothing prick you again."

"Alright fine, why do you want me to deal with this now?"

Luna stated, "If you adjust to the clothes now, then when we restart magic practice that will be one less problem we have to deal with."

Willow said, "You have a point, especially since I did not get to practice calling my wings or whatever today."

"To be honest, you summoning your wings is the least of my worries. The fact that you cast a spell in general on your first try is a sign it won't take too long for you to get the hang of your powers."

With doubt in her voice, Willow said, "If you say so."

Chapter 8

Eric's Vase

Willow packed her bag in preparation to leave the hotel. She had changed into a red tank top and acid washed jeans, one of the new outfits she had gotten earlier that day from Lunas designer. This was actually the third new outfit she had put on. Since Luna told her she would feel like she was being stuck with needles the first three times she wore the outfit, she decided to try three outfits and get it over with. The first outfit she wore she immediately felt as if her body was being poked all over by needles. Thankfully it only lasted five seconds. She then gave herself a five-minute break before trying on another outfit. The second outfit caused her the same sticking feeling as before, but thankfully it only lasted three seconds. By the time she got to the third outfit, Willow decided to change quickly into it. The needle feeling only lasted two seconds that time. Once it was over, Willow took a breath of relief.

After a few minutes Willow packed her things. As she checked to make sure she had all her stuff, she could feel her eyes tearing up. She told herself to calm down. Willow knew her tears were not from the discomfort she just endured. She was still feeling upset about all the unanswered questions in her life. Worse, she couldn't shake the feeling things were going to get a lot worse before they got better.

There was a knock on her door, followed by Luna's voice asking if she was ready. Willow took a breath then thought, *alright*

Willow, I know all this stuff is just crazy. I mean magic and your aunt being cursed is just weird. But in a way it answers a lot of questions. Even auntie's refusal to marry Uncle Eric makes more sense now. And it explains all of auntie's weird behavior, so just calm down. Things will get better. Stop expecting the worst.

She heard Luna knock on the door again asking if Willow was alright. Willow replied, "Everything's fine. I was just looking for something. I'll be ready to go in just a few minutes."

When she finished doing a final check of her room, Willow gathered her things and left the room.

Willow was driving her aunt's truck with Luna in the passenger's seat. As they pulled up to the Williams estate, Luna commented on how pretty the house was. Willow told Luna she would give her a tour of the house after dinner. She then parked the car and they both got out and went into the house.

The entrance to the Williams home had white walls and marble floors. There was a large marble staircase with black metal railing. The upstairs had doors to the left which led to guest rooms, and the entrance to the right side of the hall leading to the family's rooms. Meanwhile the lower main area had two large glass doors on the right that led to the study. On the left side were two doors with one leading to the dining room and the other leading to the kitchen. Towards the front of the room was a living area with black leather couches and a glass coffee table between them. Behind the living area was a door that led outside.

No sooner did they walk inside than they were greeted by Eric. He looked tired and was holding a coffee cup. After the usual greetings Eric said, "Dinner should be ready in thirty minutes. I have some business to handle so I might be late. If I am, don't wait for me."

"Is it that deal you mentioned a few months ago?" asked Willow.

Eric took a breath before saying, "I wish it was that. It's not a major issue, just something tedious to get out of the way. Anyway, Willow, show your friend around a little bit before dinner."

Eric told them both goodbye before heading into one of the downstairs rooms. Willow looked at Luna as she said, "Um, I guess I could show you the study first."

Luna replied, "Alright."

Willow walked over to the two glass doors and opened them. As the two of them walked into the room, Luna looked around, impressed with the surroundings. The study had dark forest green walls and the front wall was covered with bookshelves made of beautiful mahogany wood. The shelves were filled with leather bound books. On the right side of the room was a desk with a computer on top. In the center of the room was a brown leather couch with a brown end table next to it.

Willow said, "So my uncle…"

As Luna inquired why Willow paused, Willow's eyes were fixated on the nightstand next to the couch. Quickly she rushed over to it and stared at the empty surface.

Luna asked, "Is something wrong?"

"My uncle's jade vase is gone."

"Maybe he moved it."

"I don't think so. He likes having it in the study because guests are always impressed by it. Supposedly it's a part of a collection of rare jade vases, made by some master sculptor, but I forget what his name is."

"Willow, what, is that Sandy? I remember her from your encounter with her in the park. More importantly, what is she doing?"

Luna pointed to the window, and when Willow looked out. She saw Sandy running, and she was holding a bag. Willow said, "Shit, why does Sandy always want to be a problem?"

"You don't know if she is running off with the vase."

Willow, sounding determined, announced, "I'm about to find out."

Without a second thought, Willow rushed out of the house with Luna right behind her. The two of them saw Sandy run to the nearby woods. Willow knew that that area of the estate that Sandy went through led directly to the ranch where Yennifer lived.

Willow thought, *this is just too weird. Sure, Yennifer is her mom, but she would never help Sandy with anything. I wonder if those two worked out an arrangement to steal things from the house. No, no, Sandy may be acting really mean and stuff, but I don't care. There is no way she would work with that evil woman. I'll see what's really going on.*

Willow and Luna entered the wooded part of the property. The two girls had a little trouble getting through the thick woods; however, Willow was able to guide Luna out of the woods where they emerged on the ranch grounds.

The ranch had two large horse stables and an open area fenced in for horses to wander and exercise. There were a few horses grazing in the open area, but whoever was responsible for tending to them was not around. Near the right side of the fence there was a gravel road that led to a large wooden two-story house. The house had a red roof, a porch and front balcony on the second story of the house.

In a low voice Willow said, "We've got to be careful here. This is Yennifer's property, and if she catches us, she will have us arrested."

Luna whispered, "I thought your uncle keeps horses here."

"He does, but I have to get special permission to come here to ride. Without it, that bitch will call the cops on me before I can blink."

"Ok."

They soon spotted Sandy sneaking into the back of the house. They followed, but when they reached the house Willow decided not to follow Sandy inside.

Willow thought, *I can't risk Yennifer trying to charge Luna and me with breaking and entering, but I want to know what Sandy is doing here.*

Luna, who was looking inside a nearby window, said, "I don't see Sandy. Do you think she went up those stairs?"

Willow looked at the nearby staircase and said, "Crap, she probably did. We need to be careful. Upstairs is the ranch living area."

"So that's where this Yennifer person lives?"

"Yeah, I guess we have to go up there. Better yet, no, I'm being dumb. Whatever Sandy is doing here is not worth getting in trouble over. I'm sorry I dragged you here."

"I'm not. Willow can't you feel that?"

"Feel what?"

"There's a large concentration of magic coming from upstairs. It's so powerful I thought you sensed it when we got here."

"Why would there be magic here?"

"Don't know, but we need to know what it is."

Slowly the two girls walked up the stairs. When they got up to the top, Willow noticed a nearby window. The two girls looked through the window and saw a small room. The room looked like a small loft apartment. The floors and walls were wooden. There were clothes all over the floor near an unkempt metal frame bed. On the other side of the room was a dirty kitchen, complete with a sink stuffed to the brim with dirty dishes. The girls watched Sandy dig through the messy room, apparently looking for something. As Sandy seemed to be looking under the bed, Luna whispered, "She must have come here to get that vase."

Willow asked, "Why do you think that?"

Luna whispered, "I'm just assuming that because she seems to be looking for something, and I know the vase is missing."

The moment Luna finished her sentence, Sandy pulled a small blue jade vase out from under the bed. She then put the vase carefully into the bag she brought. Sandy seemed to take a sigh of relief before continuing to search under Yennifer's bed.

Willow thought, *she got the vase. What else could she be looking for?*

Sandy suddenly halted her search. She stood up quickly and seemed to be listening to something. A look of fear appeared before she raced out the back door so fast that she didn't notice Luna or Willow. Willow watched Sandy bolt for the woods dividing the two properties and then noticed that Sandy left the back door open. Carefully she closed it, only to be immediately grateful she did. Yennifer walked into the room practically skipping, followed by an angry looking Eric.

Willow thought, *why is my uncle with Yennifer? He said he had to handle an issue. I guess she's the issue.*

Eric said, "I don't know why you're so fucking happy."

Yennifer plopped down on her bed and said, "Baby, stop being grumpy."

Eric snapped, "Don't call me baby. I don't know what kind of game you're playing. But I suggest you stop now."

"Honey, I'm not trying to pull anything. I'm just glad we are finally spending a little time together."

"I'm not here to spend time with you. We have business to discuss, and I want to get this shit over with so I can go home."

Yennifer sat down on the bed and pulled down the left side of her dress, exposing part of her breast. She started to gently pat the empty space next to her while gesturing for Eric to come closer. When he didn't move, in a soft tone she said, "Why don't we have a little fun before we get down to business?"

Willow and Luna cringed, and Willow noticed Eric had a disgusted look on his face. Eric said, "Pull your top up. I'm not interested."

Yennifer not giving up, said, "Don't be shy. Come over here, sexy."

Using a cold tone of voice, Eric said, "Stop. The idea of touching you makes me want to vomit."

Yennifer frowned as she pulled her top up. She said, "Why are you being such an ass? The princess surviving the troll attack was great news. I doubt it will take long to figure out how a troll crossed into our realm."

Eric countered, "The fact that there was a troll attack at all should trouble you. As far as we know, trolls are not native to this realm, or at least Earth C157. One just popping up could mean something bad is about to happen."

Yennifer said, "The team did not find any evidence that the troll wasn't acting alone."

Eric continued, "The team could not find any information about the troll at all. The damn thing was incinerated along with anything that might have told us why it was here. That's assuming it had been carrying anything we could use for evidence to begin with."

"Eric, baby, it was a troll. Trolls aren't smart. It probably just noticed the princess when she was crossing into our realm and followed her."

"Don't call me baby, and don't lie. We both know trolls are not stupid. Those things are methodical as hell, at least most of the time. It would have been hard for Princess Luna not to notice that it followed her. The girl does not strike me as dumb enough to leave a portal open after crossing through it. The attack must have been planned."

In a cool tone Yennifer said, "If you say so. Either way, Earth C157's council got what they wanted in the end. The princess is safe, and the other little bitch had her magic awaken finally."

Eric snapped, "Don't you ever talk about Willow that way!"

In a defensive tone Yennifer said, "Fine, fine."

Eric continued, " As you know, the elders changed their minds a year ago about Willow using magic. The only problem was we didn't know how to take the seal off of her. They also were not willing to allow me to tell Martha anything until three months ago."

Willow's mind raced. *My uncle has had magic all this time? How did I not know about that? There is another magic council? Do they know what happened to my parents? Fuck, what is going on dammit?*

Yennifer said, "What, why?"

Eric answered, "I think they were worried about what Martha would do when she learned about my powers and that I have been spying on her."

Yennifer angrily said, "Dumbass, what I mean is why the fuck would they change their minds about keeping Martha in the dark about this earth's magic users? She is not from this realm. Her knowing the truth is going to result in her trying to upset things."

"That's a load of crap and you know it."

"Of course, you're too obsessed with getting that old dry pussy, to see the truth."

I wish I didn't hear her say that, thought Willow.

Eric said, "Don't shit talk my woman. My relationship with Martha has nothing to do with why I know she won't cause trouble. The only thing she cares about is keeping her family safe. Getting involved with trying to take down a government is not exactly family friendly now, is it?"

Yennifer responded, "Just wait and see. When she betrays you and you lose everything, you'll regret leaving me."

"Nothing in existence will ever make me regret ending my unhappy union with you. If you're done wasting time, let's finish what needs to be discussed. We have confirmation Princess Luna has no desire to stay in our realm for more than a month. As for Willow, the council has been waiting for years for her to use her magic. They agreed not to hurt her as long as I train her to use her magic."

"I don't get it. When your bitch and that brat came here, our job was to make sure they did not use magic. Now they want you to train the brat?"

Eric squeezed his fist as if he was holding himself back. He took a breath before continuing to say, "You are a fool. If you paid any attention all these years, you would have known the council was only fearful of them at first because they did not want war coming to this realm. But it's clear the war will never come here. Besides, if I train Willow, then there is less of a chance that she will leave the state for college."

"Why do the elders care if she leaves the state?"

Eric explained, "It's not leaving the state so much as they don't want her to go to the place where she used to live. If she ever does go, they want a member of Earth C157's magic government with her."

"Where exactly did they live in Texas?"

"I don't know. All I know is when we figure it out, they don't want her to go there alone."

Yennifer commented, "Oh, well either way, not my problem. Have the elders responded to my request?"

"I don't know why you depended on me to tell you this. But I do love bringing you news that only upsets you. Your request to remain my teammate and be granted permission to traverse the realms has been denied."

Yennifer shouted, "Dammit why?"

Eric, with some glee in his voice, said, "Same reason you were forced give me my ranch back. The elders are not happy with you. You've messed up too many missions, and you bring too much attention to yourself."

"No, I don't."

Eric countered, "Seeing that I had to bail you out of jail ten times this year… Yes, you do. Also, lose my number. After today you are no longer part of the leaders of the team, which means I will no longer be obligated to spring you out of jail. If you get arrested again and call me for help, I will laugh and let you rot in jail."

Yennifer teased, "You're nothing but talk. I know you're too good of a person to let the mother of your children sit in prison."

Eric countered, "You birthed them, but you were never a mother to them. Martha pretty much became their mother the day I hired her as a secretary. Actually, I should thank you for suggesting I hire her. Your attempt to do less work helped me to find the woman I was meant to be with."

Yennifer shouted, "FUCK YOU!"

"Whatever, bitch. The paperwork for the sale of this place has been notarized and filed. I am once again the owner of this property, which means you better be out of here by the end of the week."

"You're only giving me a week to move? That's not fair, Eric. You know I don't have any money, and I need more time to find a new home."

"Ha, it's not my problem you wasted what you got from the divorce settlement, as well as the checks you get from the magic government. I have to get this place ready to surprise my children and my fiancé. If you're not out on time I will have you arrested."

Yennifer laughed as she said, "Seriously, that woman will never marry you."

"She'll change her mind about being my wife pretty soon."

"No, she won't. You're a delusional fuck."

"That's it. I want you out by tomorrow."

"You can't do that."

Eric laughed as he said, "You're lucky I don't have you thrown out right now. It's interesting, the kids were begging me to buy this place yesterday. It's a shame I had to keep them in the dark about how I already took it from you. But they will love the fact that I had to only pay one whole dollar for it."

"GET OUT!" Yennifer screamed.

As Eric left, Yennifer grabbed a pillow and screamed into it.

Overwhelmed with what she had heard, Willow whispered, "I want to go."

"Just wait a little longer," said Luna.

"Why?"

"The magic presence in this room is really strong. I don't think it's coming from Yennifer or your uncle."

They watched Yennifer cry for about five minutes. When she stopped, she reached under her bed and pulled out a silver hand mirror. After wiping her face, she looked into the mirror, and it started to glow a bright blue.

The girls heard an eerie voice say, "What do you want now?"

Yennifer replied, "You failed to hold up your end of the deal. I told you about that princess, and you were supposed to kill Willow and Martha afterwards."

"We still haven't terminated the princess. We'll handle them after we deal with her."

"Why wait? They are all at my ex-husband's house right now."

The voice coming from the mirror said, "Taking on Princess Luna is going to be more problematic than we thought."

Luna whispered to Willow, "The mirror is what I sensed. We need to take it from her."

Willow did not see how this was possible. She whispered, "How?"

"I'm not sure, but if we can get it, then I can figure out who she's plotting with."

Yennifer said, "I don't care! The deal was you kill the bitches I asked you to kill in exchange for information about that princess."

The voice replied, "Killing Martha and Willow is more difficult than ending the princess. Eric Williams is near them almost all the time."

"So?"

"We have no desire to fight him to get to them. So, we must wait for an opportunity when he is not around."

"Worthless troll! You promised me they would die!"

The voice replied, "Screech all you want, woman. We will fulfill our end of the deal when we feel the moment is right. I suggest you have patience. Also, why haven't you left yet?"

"You sound like my ex-husband."

"Stop wasting our time. Our deal extends beyond information about the princess."

"Yeah, yeah. Just hurry up and kill those bitches for me."

The voice coming from the mirror said, "We will end them when the time is right. Stop being lazy and do your work."

Yennifer threw the mirror across the room. She snapped, "I am not letting that bitch marry my husband. If those trolls just want to play around, then I'll take the matter to someone I know will finish the job."

She then announced to herself that she needed a glass of wine. Yennifer stood and walked out of the room. When Willow and Luna were sure Yennifer was not coming back into the room, Luna opened the door. Luna walked inside Yennifer's room and was searching for the spot where the mirror landed. When she spotted it, she made a motion with her hand, and the mirror flew into her hand.

Luna left the room, closing the door behind her and locking it. Willow said, "Let's get the hell out of this place."

They snuck down the stairs before running for the woods that lead to the main house. Once they were in the woods, Willow fell to her knees. Luna touched Willow's shoulder as she asked if she was alright.

Willow looked at Luna as her eyes began to well up. She wiped her face as she said, "She wants us to die. That, that woman wants you, my aunt, and me dead."

Luna hugged her as she said, "I know, but we know what she's plotting now. Your uncle may have been keeping secrets, but I don't think he's a bad person. He'll probably help us out."

Luna let go of Willow, and Willow looked down as her hands were shaking. In a shaky voice Willow said, "I need answers now."

Suddenly both girls heard Eric say, "I would like some answers, too."

Willow's heart raced as she looked at her uncle. To her surprise he looked calm as he walked over to her. He looked at Willow as he said, "Let's get you back on your feet."

Eric helped Willow up. As soon as she was on her feet, Willow looked at him as more tears fell down her face. She said, "Uncle, she wants to kill us."

Eric replied, "I overheard you say someone was trying to hurt you, your friend, and your aunt. I also know you and Luna were spying on Yennifer and me earlier. Is Yennifer the one threatening to hurt the three of you?"

Willow wiped her eyes as she said, "Yes."

Eric paused for a moment, saying, "Why don't the three of us go inside and talk about this more. Luna, do you mind if I take a look at the mirror that you're holding?"

Chapter 9

Hidden

The dining room at the Williams estate, for the first time in Willow's life, felt unwelcoming. Like the rest of the house, the floors were covered with marble. In the center of the room was a cherry wood dining table covered with a gold tablecloth. There were twelve white chairs with gold cushions, and above the table was a large crystal chandelier.

The front wall housed the dining room entrance, and the back wall was a large window with a view of the pool. The right wall had a large fall themed painting while next to the art was a door that led to the kitchen.

Eric was sitting at the head of the table, while Willow was sitting to Eric's right, and Luna sat next to Willow. Vanessa and Pete were told to have their dinner in their rooms. Meanwhile, they were waiting for Martha and Sandy to arrive.

Willow stared down at her plate of sirloin, mashed potatoes and steamed green beans. She could feel her stomach growling, but she could not bring herself to eat. Eric, who was examining the mirror, said, "Willow, you have been through a lot today. You need to eat your dinner."

Luna, who was halfway done with her steak, said, "Your uncle's right."

Willow said, "I'm afraid of Yennifer."

Eric said, "Don't worry about Yennifer. Even before you told me what the two of you heard, I was already worried she was plotting something. I've warned her more than once of what would happen if she tried to hurt you or Martha. She is going to learn the hard way how vengeful I can be."

Willow slowly picked up her fork and ate a green bean. Meanwhile Eric put the mirror on the table next to his plate. He said, "I can't thank you both enough for getting this. I sensed some kind of powerful magic in that room, but I was not looking forward to digging through Yennifer's things to find it. The earth's council of elders has been looking for this mirror since it went missing a few months back. I wonder why Yennifer did not think I wouldn't sense the magic presence." Eric, with a tone of resignation in his voice, said, "Whatever. I will worry about it when I deal with her tomorrow."

Willow asked, "There's a council of elders? Never mind. What is the mirror for?"

Eric explained, "You can use it to communicate with people or creatures in other realms. Mirrors like this one can also be used to trap people inside it. There are a lot of criminals trapped inside of this mirror."

Willow said, "That's scary."

Eric replied, "Don't worry. Criminals can't get out of here unless someone lets them out on purpose."

"How do you know Yennifer didn't let anyone out?"

"The spell to let anyone out of this thing would release a massive shock wave that would destroy half the city. The magic power that the wave would let out can be felt by a magic user six states over."

"Whoa."

"Anyone put in the mirror is expected never to leave. Criminals in the mirror are there only because no prison can contain them, thanks to their overwhelming magical power. I'm amazed I was able to subdue a couple of the people who are trapped in this mirror."

Willow asked, "Uncle, who did you have to put in the mirror?"

"I didn't put people in the mirror. Earth C157's magic council of elders places people who are terrible in the mirror. Most of the people in here were leaders of cults. One of the people I brought in was named Sebastian Rosewood. Man, that guy is all kinds of crazy.

He believes himself to be an alien prince from another planet, who was tasked with the burden of killing ten thousand children. That belief led him to summon a daemon. What did he call that thing? Backlard. His name was Backlard. Anyway, he wanted to summon this daemon to kill all life on earth so that the planet can become pure again."

Willow responded, "I don't understand."

Eric said, "His logic never made any sense."

"Were he and his followers supposed to be the only survivors?"

Eric proceeded to tell his story. "I'm not sure. The whole thing sounds crazier every time I bring it up. When we became aware of him, he had to be stopped. His followers were easy to take out, but Sebastian was another story. He has incredible magic powers. I was partnered with several high-class spell casters. It took almost every drop of magic power we had to subdue him. Even transporting him to see the elders was a nightmare. He almost escaped twice, and it was only by the grace of God we were able to stop him."

"Wow! Um, Uncle, can you explain the council of elders?"

Eric asked, "Has the princess told you anything about the council that controls traversing the realms?"

Willow answered, "Only a little."

"Hmmm… in that case let's talk about the Earth C157's council tomorrow. I'm going to have to explain two different governments to you, and I don't want to confuse you when I do."

"Ok, but Uncle, can we just call this earth, 'earth' instead of 'earth C157'?"

Eric answered, "Not right now. I want you to have earth C157 memorized like the house address, just so you don't forget which earth you live on. Eventually you're probably going to want to traverse the realms by yourself, and you always need to remember earth C157."

"I understand. Uncle, I heard you say that you and Yennifer were on the same team. Why were you working together?"

Eric answered, "Yennifer and I are detectives for the council. Our job is to handle problems with unscrupulous magic wielders. We also hunt down and destroy monsters. Every team is composed of thirty magic wielders, and there are usually one or two team leaders for each magic defense team. Most of the time when there are two heads of a team they're married. Yennifer and I have powerful magic, so our families decided we had to marry. The council of elders agreed, and since we were married, they decided we should lead the same team."

Willow said, "Uncle, that makes no sense. I get that you both have strong magic and stuff, but you two don't work well together. I never forgot how bad things were when you two were in charge of the pre-school bake sale. When the two of you weren't arguing with one another, Yennifer was throwing baked goods at you."

Eric said in bewilderment, "Why do you remember that? You can't remember me taking you, Sandy, and Vanessa to that princess world tea house later that day?"

Willow laughed, "I guess that fight was too memorable. Yennifer was so scary I thought she was going to murder you."

"Like you said, having strong magic and being married to someone with strong magic doesn't make someone good at a job. I had to hit the ground running trying to learn the best way to lead my team. Meanwhile, Yennifer was no help and would frequently abandon her duties."

"Why was she begging to remain a team leader if she does not want to do her job?"

Eric answered, "The pay is good, and she enjoys flirting with me. She has some delusional idea that we will get back together, which she only wants to do because she has spent all of the money that she gained during our divorce."

"I understand. Um, Uncle, if you don't mind me asking- why did you marry Yennifer?"

"My parents signed a contract with Yennifer's family, agreeing to have my magic removed if I did not go through with it."

"That's mean. Why do you have to agree to follow their contract?"

"It's legal because the magic government allows parents to make contracts like that. The council believes that allowing parents of children with strong magical abilities to make contracts like that will lead to more children being born with powerful magic. Only one parent has to agree to make the contract. I knew Yennifer would make a contract with a powerful magic family for Sandy, Vanessa, and Pete if she knew they had magic.

When each of them was born she had no desire to hold them, granting me the opportunity to seal their magic without her knowledge. Sandy's magic reached a point where it got stronger than my spell. She broke it unknowingly, and Yennifer discovered that

Sandy had magical powers. However, Yennifer never realized Sandy always had magic. She believes Sandy is a bloom egg, which is a person whose magic shows up later in life. Fortunately, Sandy was eighteen when Yennifer found out she had magic. Since Sandy was legally an adult, Yennifer could not try to get a contract on her."

Willow said, "I think I understand, but Uncle, if it's possible to remove someone's magic, why waste time with that mirror?"

"Not everyone's magic can be removed. Also, successful magic removal can lead to a person becoming a vegetable."

Luna said, "That's why most realms that we know of made magic removal illegal."

Eric continued, "Speaking of illegal, it's illegal to plot to kill someone. It's also illegal to help trolls come here. When the council learns Yennifer was involved in that incident with the troll in the park attack, they might put her in this mirror."

Luna said, "Now that you bring up the troll, how long did you know about that?"

Eric answered honestly. "Ten minutes before you and Willow arrived at Martha's house, I got a call from one of my subordinates about a troll attack. That's when I learned about you and how Willow accidentally set the park on fire."

Luna took a sip of water from her glass. She said, "Ok, why didn't your subordinate help me fight the troll?"

"Yennifer was responsible for spying on you when you arrived here. I didn't trust her with the task, but there was nothing I could do. She went to the council and begged them to let her do the job on her own. Yennifer has a friend on the council who vouched for her, and her request was granted.

I'm not willing to risk someone getting hurt or having problems with another realm because that lazy woman wants to pretend to do a job. So, I had one of my subordinates follow her. I also had someone tail Princess Luna, but that person was attacked a few minutes before the troll attack. I don't know who attacked them, but I did not learn about the attack until I was informed about the troll attack." Eric explained, "which I learned from a different subordinate who was checking in on the one who was following Luna."

Luna asked, "Mr. Williams, where was Yennifer when I was attacked?"

"She was at a night club, getting drunk and high."

Willow said, "She was probably celebrating that deal she made with the trolls."

Eric said, "It's lucky Willow found you, and just as lucky Willow was able to break the seal on her magic to save both of you."

Willow said, "Did you seal my magic?"

Eric replied, "No, I didn't, and I don't know who did. I think your Aunt Martha knows, but thanks to the curse she can't tell me."

"Ok. Um, Uncle, why didn't you say anything when I brought Luna to my aunt's house?"

"I thought it would be better to wait and have you invite Luna here. Telling you we had magic after you had time to accept that magic exists would ease the blow."

"Ok, I guess already knowing about magic helped. So, what do you plan to do about Yennifer?"

"Handling Yennifer has been in the works long before I learned she was plotting to hurt you, because she was hurting Sandy."

Willow said, "Why? Wait, forget I asked that question."

"I know Sandy has been unpleasant to be around for a while. It's not her fault she acted that way, it's mine. I should have immediately figured out when Sandy started acting strange that Yennifer was involved. As you know, Yennifer, your aunt, Sandy, Vanessa, and Pete have magic. My staff for the house and my staff at my company have magic as well."

Willow, in a whispered tone, said, "Miss Felicia has magic, and I'm guessing Uncle Thomas has magic as well?"

Eric answered, "Yes, they do. As I said before, I sealed all my children's powers when they were born. As for my staff, I have to periodically use my powers to cloak their magic. There are a lot of high-level magic users with the same ability on Earth C157. That's why the council who manages realms thinks there are no magic wielders here."

"Wow," said Luna.

Willow asked, "Why hide magic wielders from the council?"

Eric answered, "The council who monitors realms is dangerous. If they knew there were magic and non-magic users here, they would forcibly segregate the population between magic and non-magic people. This is done by forcing the entire non-magic population to live in secluded areas. They would also forcibly keep their non-magical population low."

Luna said, "He's right. They do messed up stuff like that."

Willow asked, "Why?"

Luna said, "They don't like magic and non-magic people mixing."

Willow replied, "Oh, so this is some fascist mess."

Eric said, "Yes, that is exactly what we are dealing with. But the council of Earth C157 is not that much better. They don't like magic and non-magic people mixing either. They just have no desire to subjugate non-magical people, just keep magic hidden and separated from people without it."

Luna asked, "So how did that Yennifer person find out Sandy has magic? I know you said Sandy broke the seal that you had placed on her at birth. But it's strange Yennifer would know before you or your staff, seeing how she no longer lives here."

Eric said, "Yennifer snuck into the house late one night and unfortunately it was the night Sandy managed to break my spell."

Luna asked, "Why did she sneak in?"

Willow answered, "Yennifer does that sometimes to steal stuff."

Luna replied, "Oh right, that's why your uncle's vase was at Yennifer's place."

Eric took a breath as he said, "My vase was what? Never mind, let me explain from the beginning. I was not home when Sandy's powers re-awakened. Yennifer took advantage of Sandy's confusion and used it to make her think I would disown her if I found out. Then she blackmailed Sandy to get involved with selling drugs, trying to manipulate men with money, and making Sandy distance herself from all of us."

Willow thought, *I thought Sandy had changed. This whole time that evil woman was manipulating her.*

Eric continued, "I only began to figure things out when Sandy came back from school. When she was acting bizarre near the end of high school, I foolishly believed that since she was turning eighteen that it was just a phase. When she came home announcing she had dropped out of school, I was suspicious. I contacted her college only to discover she was never kicked out. Her grades were all A's, and Sandy apparently transferred to an online school. She's even close to getting a fine arts degree in a few months. I confronted her about this and got her to tell me the truth.

Once I learned what happened, I was amazed that I never sensed that Sandy's magic was unsealed. Yennifer apparently taught her how to hide her magic. I'm impressed Sandy is so talented at hiding her powers. After I made Sandy aware that I already knew she had magic, I realized I didn't want Yennifer to know I knew she was blackmailing our daughter."

Willow asked, "Why not? I don't see any benefit to that."

Eric said, "As you discovered, Yennifer is involved in a lot of unsavory things. My team is talented but sadly so is Yennifer, at least when she wants to apply herself. So, Sandy continued to be mean for the sake of deceiving Yennifer. Sadly, I did not foresee that she would have to do so for over three months."

"Does Aunt Martha know?" Willow asked.

Eric answered, "She found out when I took her on that trip. I got permission to tell your aunt the truth. The whole point of the trip was to make it easier for me to talk her into not leaving me when she learned the truth. I figured if I showed her a good time it would soften her rage. I was more than a little wrong."

Willow asked, "So that's why she wouldn't talk to you when you guys got back?"

"Yes, to be honest, you're handling this better than she did."

"Uncle, I think I'm handling this entire situation ok because I'm finally getting some answers to questions I've always had. Although, if Sandy being a lazy college dropout was a ruse, then what was with her blasting music to stay awake? Also, why has she gotten so thin?"

"She's not getting thinner I just cast a spell to make her look like that. Yennifer is trying to have Sandy work herself to death. Why I still don't know. As for the music, she was playing loud music to stay awake so she could finish her assignments. I keep telling her that doing that is not effective, but she won't listen. I've warned her if she keeps doing that, I'm taking away her stereo."

Martha walked into the room. She immediately rushed over to Willow and hugged her. In a tearful voice she said, "I'm so sorry, Willow. I should have tried harder to tell you the truth, so you wouldn't have to have found out the way you did."

Willow replied, "It's okay, Auntie. I know you wanted to tell me about this magic stuff. Uncle Eric and the council and whoever it was who put a curse on you, are responsible for keeping me in the dark."

Martha let go of Willow before introducing herself to Luna and sitting down next to Eric. She said, "I'm glad you know I didn't keep you in the dark because I wanted to."

Willow replied, "Knowing how hard you tried to tell me at dinner the other night, I know you wanted to tell me the truth. But now that I know the truth I'm scared of Yennifer. She and uncle had a fight. After he left, she threatened to hurt me, you, and Luna. Uncle says not to worry about her, but I'm afraid."

Martha said, "She what?" Then she turned to look at Eric and asked, "Why were you talking to that woman?"

Eric told Martha about everything, except his acquisition of the ranch. Martha looked at Eric with a blank stare for a moment. Then she grabbed her steak knife and told everyone she would be back in a few hours. In response, Eric jumped up and quickly rushed over to scoop Martha into his arms.

"Let me go!" Martha demanded.

Eric responded, "Baby, I can't let you kill her."

Martha, with anger in her voice, said, "She is trying to kill Willow, me, and the princess. She put Sandy through hell for over a year and sent that troll after the princess. Willow and Princess Luna could have died!"

"Martha, I know Yennifer is horrible. But my plan to get revenge on her is about to be put into motion. We will have the last laugh soon. Also, you have no idea where Yennifer is. Just be a little patient instead of wandering the streets all night trying to find her."

"She is probably at that cheap bar she frequents."

Eric said, "She got banned from there."

"How do you know?"

"I had to bail her out of jail after the owner called the cops on her, remember?"

Calming down, Martha said, "Oh right, fine, I'll be patient. But if you don't handle her by tomorrow, I'm going to handle things myself."

Eric stated, "That's fair."

"Can you please put me down now?"

"I don't want to."

"Eric!"

Complying with Martha's request, Eric in a playful tone, said, "Alright."

After setting Martha back on her feet, Eric asked, "Where is Sandy?"

Martha said, "Sandy won't be joining us. She seems tired, but she is determined to finish her thesis on Marcel Duchamp."

Eric asked, "Is her dinner being brought up to her?"

Martha replied, "Yes."

Martha sat down next to Eric who rang a small bell to signal the staff to bring Martha her dinner. Eric then explained to Martha what he told Willow and Luna. Martha looked at Willow and said, "There is a lot we need to talk about."

Eric said, "Let me do most of the explaining. I'm worried the curse will freak you out if you try to say too much. But let me know if I get any details wrong."

Martha said, "Alright."

Eric said, "Willow, you probably already guessed this, but you're not from this realm. I don't know which one because Martha can't tell me. She came here to protect you from someone who was after you. What they want, I don't know, but I am planning to find answers in Texas."

Willow said, "You are going to Texas?"

Martha and Eric laughed as Eric said, "We knew about your plot to go to Texas. You can't trick us that easily. But I understand your determination, and you deserve answers."

Eric said, "And you are not getting a rental car. I just told you I would help you rent one to stall for a little bit. I'm also still punishing you for thinking you could trick me, so I'm not giving you your car till the end of the summer. Lastly, you're not going to get a black Amex credit card till your second year of college."

Willow said, "You were going to give me a black Amex card?"

"Yes, but now you are going to have to get through your first year of college with a monthly allowance of two hundred dollars, which means you better think about finding a job."

"But Uncle…"

"But uncle, nothing, you do not try to deceive me. You're lucky you're eighteen, so legally I can't ground you. I can and did ground

Vanessa for a month for going along with what you were plotting. Willow, I know the two of you want answers, but you were going about it in the wrong way."

Willow took a breath as she said, "Ok. I guess I'll be letting my friends know we are not going."

"Lastly, Willow, you are not going to Texas. My team and I are."

Willow insisted, "Uncle, I really want to go."

Eric continued, "I know, but I don't think it is safe for you to go. Whoever attacked you and Martha may still be there."

"I understand."

Reassuring Willow, Eric said, "Don't worry. I will let you know what I discover. Right now, there are three places in that state I believe the two of you were living. I am going to head there at the end of the week because I need to deal with Yennifer first."

Luna asked, "Is it alright if I stay here until you get the answers you're searching for? I have a sick feeling that all of this is connected to the mess with the trolls."

Eric replied, "We are more than happy to have you. To be honest, I'm worried another troll may try to hurt you. Also, from the little I know about this, your assumption may be right. Or Yennifer is the only connecting factor. I'm not sure yet."

Willow asked, "Uncle, why do you think all of this is connected?"

Eric answered, "Trolls always scout out an area before they attack. They will not attack if someone they don't want to see them wanders in. The troll you faced was hoping that you would stumble upon him."

Luna said, "Remember the troll did say something like the second rat is finally here."

Martha said, "He said that?"

Luna replied, "Something along those lines."

Martha replied, "Oh shit."

Willow looked at her aunt as she asked, "What's wrong?"

Martha replied, "We may be out of time."

Willow started to inquire as to what her aunt meant; however, Martha had a look of pure terror.

Eric said, "Martha don't answer. Princess Luna, Martha can't give us a clear idea of who she is talking about because of her curse. She has been trying to allude to some evil coming all day. I'm not sure when this person will show up, but I have increased the house defenses."

Luna replied, "Alright, and please just call me Luna."

"Alright," Eric replied.

Martha said, "Preparing the house is, is, is dammit."

Eric said, "Martha don't strain yourself by trying to tell us more information."

"Damn that curse," Willow said.

Eric replied, "Your aunt is actually under three different curses. One makes her experience overwhelming fear if she tries to talk about her life before San Francisco. The second and third I have no idea what they do, I just know they're there."

Luna said, "I think I know how the first curse can be removed, but it's tricky."

Martha said, "I know what you're talking about. We, we can't even a, a, attempt to remove it."

Willow asked, "Why not?"

Eric answered, "We would first have to figure out which realm you and Martha come from." He continued, "which will not be easy since she can't tell us. The only clues to help us seem to be in Texas."

Willow and Luna sat alone at the table. Luna said, "Wow, that was a lot."

Willow replied, "Why do you think the troll problem is interconnected?"

"I've been bothered by the troll attacking you. I didn't want to mention it sooner because I wanted to get to know you a little better, to get a better idea of what kind of person you are. The trolls more than likely sent the troll that attacked me to try to steal my power. I think that troll suspected you would come across us. Then, it would kill both of us and get what it was after. I suspect the trolls want more than my magic, and the trolls probably made a deal with Yennifer because they want your power as well."

"You think I have some kind of secret power?"

Luna said, "I don't know if it's a secret, because your aunt can't tell us what's going on. I hate fear curses. Those are some of the hardest to break."

"I know my uncle says he has got the situation under control, but the way my aunt was acting has me thinking he's wrong."

Luna commented, "She was acting a little extreme about you learning a few defense spells after dinner. Something is definitely about to happen, and the only person who knows can't tell us."

Willow said, "This is frustrating."

Just then Sandy walked in. She greeted Luna and asked Willow if she could talk for a minute. Willow excused herself, telling Luna she would come back in a few minutes. Sandy and Willow went into Eric's study. As soon as they entered the room Sandy said, "I know I've been a…"

Willow interrupted, "You don't need to apologize. I forgive you. It must have been tough."

"Thank you, Willow. I was fearful that when the truth came out the family wouldn't believe me."

Using a reassuring tone, Willow said, "Sandy, we are family, and in this family we are here for one another."

They hugged as Willow thought, *I've got my big sister back.*

Sandy said, "Speaking of family, why were you and your friend Luna at Yennifer's place?"

Willow asked, "You saw us?"

Sandy responded, "Yeah, I'm not blind. I figured you both were spying on her for some reason. But my main concern was getting dad's vase out of her place before she came back. I'm lucky you and your friend found the mirror. I sensed a powerful magic item, but as you saw I didn't have time to get it."

Willow confessed, "To be honest we were following you. I thought you stole the vase."

"I understand. You know, she had the nerve to demand I steal the vase."

Willow remembered when she heard Sandy on the phone the other day. She said, "When I saw you at the house, I heard you arguing with someone. I thought it was Yennifer, but I wasn't sure."

Sandy said, "I guessed that you heard my conversation with her. I still had to keep up the act. But when Yennifer called me demanding I steal dad's entire jade collection, I figured the whole mess was at an end and I really couldn't handle the situation anymore. For almost four years I had to pretend to be a jackass. I don't even get how pretending to have an attitude problem was beneficial to her. No, I take that back. I don't think she wants me to be successful. I missed out on going to the college I wanted to because I had to let my grades suffer my senior year. I missed out on family trips and other family stuff. I missed out on a lot of college experiences because I had to act like a bitch and do stuff for her. Shit, I even had to date that asshole, Sam."

"Why did she want you to date Sam?"

"He belongs to an influential magic family. For some reason she thought I could get him to marry me. That way she could use me to benefit from his family's power and influence and as a way of getting her hands on his money."

Willow said with a question in her voice, "Wait, if he belongs to a magic family then… oh shit. My friend Darrell must have magic."

Sandy said, "Maybe he does if he's related to your friend. But I have to say, Sam is just a bastard. I had to pretend to be high all the time when I spent time with him. Worse, I had to drug the jackass. I take that back, he deserved it."

"What, why?"

"He tried to slip me a Mickey several times. I was onto him and used magic to switch our drinks."

"Oh, wait, why did you pretend to be a junky at home?"

"If Miss Martha and dad didn't think I was a junkie, then Yennifer was going to tell dad about my magic. She has me casting spells on video. When I first discovered my magic, Yennifer told me I inherited her family's powers. Then she gave me some story about how dad hated magic. She said he believed it was the calling of the devil, and people born with it were cursed. I was so freaked out about having magic that I bought her story. She also had me thinking she didn't have magic. She gave me a few old spell books claiming they were ancient text that had been in her family for generations. They were actually dad's old textbooks!"

"Was there an indicator on the book showing that?"

Sandy said, "No, all my dad's old textbooks are old and leather-bound with discolored pages. When I first saw them, I thought it was so cool I was getting some kind of ancient text. After my dad found out he told me all magic textbooks are made to look like that, something about the older they look the more expensive they are.

Sandy continued to tell her story. "Anyway, Yennifer filmed me practicing learning how to use my powers and that's when the blackmail started. I'm glad that when I dropped out of school dad became suspicious. Actually, I didn't drop out. I transferred."

"I know, your dad told me."

"I'm just glad I get to be myself around everybody now. Acting the way she wanted me to be was tiresome."

Willow said, "I'm still amazed you were able to keep that act up for so long. What's more impressive is that you fooled everybody."

Sandy giggled as she said, "Dad and Miss Martha told me I should go into acting. They are still impressed that I was able to trick them for a little over three years."

"They have a point."

"Yeah, but after all this I'm tired of acting."

Just then Eric walked in and said, "Willow, I've got the back yard set up to teach you some defense spells."

Willow, Sandy, Luna, and Eric stood on the back yard patio. The outdoor furniture had been removed. Willow always loved spending time sitting by and swimming in the pool area. There were lights in the bottom of the pool that changed colors, reminding Willow of a kaleidoscope.

Eric looked at the pool and said, "I really need to swap those lights out in the pool."

In unison all three women said, "No."

Eric replied, "If you don't want me to change it, Willow, then you have to master all three defense spells."

Willow answered, "Uncle, there's no way you're going to spend all that money to take the lights out just because I don't master a spell right away."

Eric laughed as he replied, "Willow, I have billions in the bank. I also have much, much more in Switzerland and the Cayman Islands. Don't ever believe I'm above compulsive household spending.

Let's begin. First, I'm going use the pool water to launch a few orbs of water at you. You will need to destroy the orbs before they hit you. The spell you will learn to destroy the orbs is called bisttowere. It is an effective light magic spell that can destroy incoming projectiles. Sadly, it's one of the weaker protection spells, so you have to target the spell at each projectile one at a time."

"Uncle, can't I just learn a spell that lets me block all the objects at once?"

Eric, sharing information, stated, "I'm going to teach you one dark magic spell that does just that. I'm starting with the bisttowere spell because dark magic spells tend to be more powerful. It will drain more of your magic energy. If you had had years of experience or were a pure dark magic fairy type, then I would start you off with dark magic and then teach you some light magic."

"Uncle, I'm confused."

"At dinner you mentioned Luna told you about magic types, and a little about dark and light magic. Magic is more complicated than being a Fairy, Witch, Elf, etcetera. Magic types are in your DNA. For example, when I did my DNA test, I learned I was sixty percent Ghanian, thirty percent Senegalese, twenty percent Mali, four percent Ethiopian, and six percent Spanish. The same way people tend to have a mixed batch in their DNA, you can be a mixed batch of magic types."

Willow questioned, "Luna ran a basic test on me to determine my magic type, but the results were inconclusive, except it indicated that not only was I a Fairy but a mix of other types of magic casters. Is that from different magic groups intermarrying?"

Eric remarked, "Yes, and I ran a more detailed test on you when you were I think eight."

Willow wondered aloud, "How did I not notice that?"

"You lost one of your back teeth and Martha was too sleepy to play tooth fairy. After this tooth fairy left you twenty bucks, I used your tooth to run some tests on you."

Sandy asked, "Daddy, why were you such a cheap tooth fairy? When Mama Martha did it, she gave us fifty. Unless it was a front tooth, then it was a hundred."

Eric scoffed then said, "Excuse me, kid, you're lucky I didn't leave you a quarter. Also, how did you learn about that?"

"Mama Martha told me. I was fifteen and for some reason I was curious about the whole tooth fairy thing."

Eric, perplexed, stated, "I'll never understand Martha's obsession with keeping all you kids' baby teeth. She got more than a little pissed at me when I told her I lost the tooth I tested."

Luna asked, "Why did you tell her you lost it?"

Eric answered, "Teeth don't survive the test. I couldn't tell her that I was a magic user. So, I said I lost it. We are getting off track. Willow, when I tested your tooth, I learned you were a fairy and dragon type but…"

"I'm part dragon?!" screeched Willow.

At the same time, Luna fell to her knees. She looked at Willow as she said "Dragon, oh my god. You're a dragon. That is so epic!"

Eric took a breath then said, "Yes, I realize now the basic test did not make it clear to Luna that Willow has dragon magic."

Luna said, "This must be the reason why Miss Martha had to run away with Willow. Dragon magic wielders are powerful and rare."

"Wow," said Sandy.

Eric replied, "I think that was part of the reason, but dragon magic is hard to control. Unlike other magic, it can't be extracted. Also, it can only be taught by the person you inherited it from. I ran a secret test on Martha, and she is only a fairy. She and Willow's mother have the same parents. So, I can conclude that Willow you must have gotten your dragon magic from your father. I'm not sure how Willow having dragon magic plays into any of this, and I need to stop speculating reasons. It's late, and I have to teach you three spells. Willow, if you want to keep fancy pool lights, then you better master these spells."

Willow asked, "But you were explaining specifics about magic types."

"I'll tell you more tomorrow. I promise. Let's get started."

Sandy said, "Dad, are you sure we should do this now? I just checked the time, and it is almost eleven."

Eric replied, "Yes, it's better to learn defense spells when you're tired and under stress. It makes using these types of spells more of a reflex when necessary. Let's start with a demonstration."

Eric made a motion with his hands, and a large ball of water rose out of the pool. He then motioned towards Sandy, and the ball of water raced towards her. Sandy quickly pointed at the ball of water, and she said, "Bisttowere".

Instantly the water ball disappeared. Eric summoned three more balls of water and launched them at his daughter. Sandy quickly pointed at each of them and repeated the spell. Each time the water disappeared.

Eric looked at Willow and said, "It's your turn. Remember how Sandy performed the spell."

Willow felt her heart race as Eric summoned a ball of water. When he launched it at her, she pointed at the water ball and shouted, "Bisttowere!"

The ball started to fizzle and quickly evaporated. Willow smiled and said, "I did it."

Luna looked at Willow and said, "Actually you didn't, but that was a nice first attempt."

Willow's smile disappeared as she said, "But I made the water disappear."

Sandy replied, "You made it quickly evaporate. The point of this spell is to make an incoming projectile disappear. If you make the object fizzle away, then there is a chance the spell won't fully catch what was headed towards you. Don't stress about it. You've never done this spell before."

Eric said, "Let's try again."

Before Willow could blink, Eric already had another water ball racing toward her. She fumbled the words for the spell as she pointed at the water ball. The ball exploded, splashing Willow. Willow looked at herself noticing she was completely drenched. Eric said, "Don't worry about it."

He snapped his fingers, and suddenly Willow noticed that her clothes were dry. Before she could ask how he did that, Eric had already sent another water ball her way. Willow quickly pointed and shouted, "Bisttowere!"

This time the water disappeared, but before Willow could celebrate, Eric had already launched another ball of water at her. Willow performed the spell again, and the water ball vanished. Eric then sent four balls of water at Willow, and she was able to make all four disappear.

The moment the four water balls disappeared, Eric said, "Good, I didn't expect you to get those. Now that I say that aloud I probably should have."

"Why?" asked Willow.

Eric replied "Your aunt took you to the shooting range more times than I would like. You're already good at targeting."

"I forgot about that."

"It has been a while since the two of you went. Stay on your toes."

Before Willow could think, she was slammed in the face by a water ball. As she wiped the water from her eyes, she was hit by two more water balls. She thought, *he's not going to go easy on me. I can't blame him. I need to master this spell like breathing.*

Three balls of water headed toward Willow. This time she was ready and made all three water balls disappear. Eric kept launching so many balls of water at Willow that she thought he was going to empty the pool. Eventually he stopped and Willow fell down, exhausted.

Eric said, "I think you have that spell down. Time to move on."

He waved his hand and Willow's clothes were suddenly dry. Eric said, "This next spell is going to be more challenging. It is a front shield spell. I would have liked you to start off with a full body shield. Sadly, front body shield spells are the best for when you are at your limit. You can maintain this spell for longer. To do this spell you have to hold your arms forward, with your palms facing forward, and say, "sibenlo" as loud as you can in your head."

Willow said, "Ok, but why do I have to think this one instead of saying it?"

"This is one of the few spells where you can practice it without saying it aloud first. One day you won't have to verbalize any of your spells. Alright, Sandy and Luna will demonstrate."

Luna suddenly shouted, "slpolops!"

Orbs of light materialized. The orbs bolted at Sandy, who had her hands and arms outstretched. Each orb hit what looked like an invisible barrier.

Eric said, "Alright, Willow, your turn. Willow shouted the spell in her mind as she had her hand and arms outstretched. Luna sent orbs of light hurtling towards her. All the orbs of light hit an invisible barrier. Willow was about to put her arms down when Luna started to shoot more light orbs at her.

As Luna kept shooting orbs at her, Willows arms began to hurt. Fear of the orbs hitting her provoked her not to drop her arms. Sandy said, "Sorry, Willow, but you have to do this for a while. You never know if you will end up in a situation where you must shield yourself for a long time."

When Luna finally stopped, she and Willow fell to the ground exhausted. Eric said, "You both did a great job. Alright, Willow, time for the last spell."

Willow asked, "Uncle, can I have five minutes?"

"No, it's better for you to practice these spells while you're tired. The last spell is a dark magic spell. It reflects any spell sent your way, back at the spell caster. For this spell you have to shout, "Relimaw."

"Relimadf?"

"No, relimaw."

"Relimaw?"

"Yes, that's correct. Let's begin."

Eric shot a ball of water at Willow as she shouted, "Relimaw!"

The ball shot back at Eric who, without flinching, sent it back towards Willow. Willow shouted the spell again, sending the ball flying back to Eric. Once again Eric sent the water ball her way, and she sent it back again. Eventually Eric shot the ball back into the pool.

Willow tried to catch her breath. All the magic practice she had just completed felt like an intense physical and mental workout. She said, "That was intense."

Eric shrugged as he said, "You three should get some rest. We have a lot to do in the morning."

As everyone started to head inside, Felicia walked out and said, "Eric, you need to speak with Vanessa and Pete about their magic."

Eric asked, "Why? I wasn't going to tell them until morning."

Felicia explained, "That may be what you wanted to do, but Pete saw a little bit of that magic practice. Then naturally he went to Vanessa and showed her what was happening."

Eric questioned, "How? They're supposed to be in the basement watching that robot movie."

Frustration in her voice, Felicia said, "Eric Williams, I tried to handle the situation as best I could so you could train Willow, but I'm an old woman and I'm tired. Will you please deal with your children?"

"Ok, ok. I will handle things."

Willow lies awake in her room. Her room at the Williams estate was much larger than the one at her aunt's house. The room had white carpeted floors, and the walls were painted a light purple color. There was a white couch on the left side of the room in between two white doors. One door led out of the room while the other door led to Willow's bathroom. The front wall housed a large tv while the left wall was home to a large window covered by white curtains. Willow's sleigh bed with gray sheets sat near the back wall.

As Willow lay on her bed staring at the ceiling, her mind felt crowded with thoughts of the events of the last twenty-four hours that had forever changed her life. She was proud of the fact that she had been able to cast all the spells her uncle taught her, but something felt off. *I don't think auntie wanted me to learn those spells just because of Yennifer. I don't know why, but ever since I came back in this house, I feel odd, as if something is coming and I need to be ready for it.* There was a knock at her door. Willow told whoever it was to come in.

Martha walked in carrying two mugs. She said, "I thought tonight is definitely a cinnamon cocoa night."

Willow sat up as she took a mug from Martha. She thanked her aunt before taking a sip of cocoa. The sweet taste of the cocoa had a calming effect on Willow. Willow said, "Cocoa always makes me feel better."

Martha said, "I'm not surprised. You have a sweet tooth like your father. I'm referring to your mother's boyfriend. The older you get the more you look like him."

"He liked sweet things?"

"I wish I could tell you more, but I know the curse won't let me. There is so much I need to tell you, so much you need to prepare for, and we don't have a lot of time."

"Can you at least tell me why we haven't gone to Texas before?"

"Sorry, I can't. The curse won't allow it. I'm lucky you ran into your new friend, otherwise your magic wouldn't have broken the seal that was put on you."

"Did you seal my magic?"

"No, and I can't tell you who did."

"Was my magic sealed to protect me?"

"No, please stop asking me about why your magic was sealed. I can already feel that this curse won't allow me to say more."

"Oh, ok. Um, can we talk about Uncle Eric and his magic powers?"

Martha said, "Sure, that is a subject I admit I'm still a little irritated about. He invites me on a romantic vacation just to spring on me the fact that he has magic. Worse, he's been spying on us. I think the whole point of the vacation was so I wouldn't break up with him and storm off." With anger in her voice, Martha stated, "Shady son of a bitch."

Willow asked, "You're still mad?"

"Of course, I'm mad! I just figured if I don't want to break up with him, then I need to process and let go of my anger. Although Eric's fear that I'm going to break up with him at any moment does not help things. It only complicates our relationship on so many levels."

"Why is he still fearful that you will end your relationship?"

Martha answered, "Pumpkin, he dropped a bombshell on me. I can forgive him only because the lying and the spying was not something he wanted to do. I'm not completely innocent either. After all, I was hiding my magic from him. Even though he already knew the truth, your uncle took me on that trip for three reasons: to tell me he had magic, to let me know the truth about Sandy, and to let me know about Earth C157's magic council. He told me the truth on the last day we were on the trip, out of fear. At first his plan was to tell me the truth in a different country so I would not run away from him.

When he finally did tell me the truth, he revealed that he was both a dark and light magic fairy type, which surprised me. I wasn't so much surprised from learning he had magic, because when in the past I sometimes sensed powerful magic coming from him, I brushed it off thinking that it was part of my curse, that I was projecting onto him my own magical abilities. When he told me the truth, and I sensed how powerful his magic is, I thought he would be more than a two-spell type."

"Can you explain the whole dark and light magic thing?"

Martha continued, "Sorry, but he will have to explain that to you. Anyway, after he told me the truth, I couldn't handle being around him for a while. He's been secretly monitoring us for years, and Yennifer was supposed to help him do it. Apparently, it all started when we came here. There are magic council offices practically everywhere, hidden in plain sight. But there was not one in place in Texas where we lived when I brought us here. When we came from San Francisco I used a portal to bring us here. The moment I set foot in this city, Earth C157's magic council knew I was here.

I can't tell you much, but your auntie is one powerful fairy. So, Earth C157's magic council sent your uncle and Yennifer to get close to us and monitor us. Your uncle is apparently the third most powerful magic wielder in the city, and Yennifer is the fifth most powerful. Like every other realm, I'm aware of how powerful magic families arrange marriages for their children so that they marry someone with strong magic. All marriages are handled through Earth C157's magic council."

Willow stated, "Uncle told me about that. It made their marriage make so much sense."

Willow looked at her cocoa as she said "Auntie, I found a key with a Texas address attached to it in our house. Is it the key to our place in Texas?"

"No, I don't know anything about that. Do you have it now?"

"No, it's in my room at our place."

"I have to look at it when we go back to the house."

With sadness in her voice, Willow said, "Auntie, all I've ever wanted is the truth about my mom and dad. But now I think I'm afraid of the answer."

Martha speaking frankly to Willow stated, "I admit all of this terrifies me as well. Not just because the curse forces me to feel fear from anything that has to do with my past, but I've worked so hard for so long to try to keep us hidden. But even before your friend arrived, I knew we would not be able to hide from the past for much longer. We are going to have to go back to Texas soon whether I like it or not. I'm just not sure how many days we have left."

"What do you mean? Uncle said he is leaving at the end of the week."

Martha said, "I wish I could explain it to you and tell your uncle about it, but unfortunately I can't do anything but leave breadcrumbs."

Feeling that her aunt was being deliberately mysterious, Willow questioned, "Auntie, I don't understand what you mean."

"You'll know the answer soon enough."

Chapter 10

Welcome Home

The sun had barely poked its head above the horizon as Willow rolled out of bed. No sooner was she on her feet than she wanted to climb back in bed. She had just experienced the worst night of her life. She had awakened several times in a cold sweat, feeling as if someone were trying to grab her. She knew it was just her nerves overreacting to the conversation she had had with her aunt. Willow forced herself to get up and take a shower. After changing into one of her new magical outfits and feeling exhausted, Willow lay back on her bed.

She thought, *normally I feel better after a shower. Instead, I think I feel worse. Auntie was so cryptic last night about there not being much time left. What does that even mean? Is whoever this guy that she's scared of, going to be here soon? I only mastered three defensive spells, how am I going to be able to fight against…*

There was a knock on her door interrupting Willow's thoughts. Shocked by the sudden sound, Willow sat up in her bed and looked around her room. There was a second knock on her door. This time she heard Felicia's voice telling her to come down for breakfast. After rolling out of bed, Willow dragged herself to the bedroom door. As she reached for the handle, she heard Vanessa scream. Willow's heart leaped, and without a second thought she raced out of her room, searching for Vanessa. Vanessa screamed again and the sound seemed to come from the front of the house.

Willow reached the main area where she saw Vanessa and Sandy. Sandy snapped, "Stop screaming!"

Vanessa replied, "But, but you said you're a fairy."

Sandy said, "Why does that surprise you? Dad told you all of this last night. You have magic as well. Your magical powers are just sealed."

Vanessa asked, "How do I unseal them?"

Sandy replied, "You don't, and if Yennifer finds out she'll force you into an arranged marriage."

Vanessa remarked, "But, but you can use your powers."

Sandy explained, "I'm legally an adult. So, Yennifer can't force me into an unwanted relationship, although that didn't stop her from trying."

"Now that I have all the information, you dating that playboy does make more sense now. I am still perplexed why Yennifer believed that guy would have been a good husband for you."

Sandy answered, "She doesn't think things through."

Eric walked over to the pair and asked what all the screaming was about. When Vanessa told him why she screamed, he folded his arms. Eric said, "Vanessa, I understand you need time to adjust to what you learned, but little girl, you need to stop screaming."

Vanessa said, "I'm sorry, Daddy. I guess I wasn't expecting Sandy to confirm what you told Pete and me."

Eric continued, "I understand suddenly learning you are a member of a magical family and that you have magical powers is a lot to accept. But you need to calm down. I do not know what Yennifer is planning; however, I do know if she or her parents learn the truth about you and your brother, then they will exploit you both."

Vanessa took a breath and then said, "I understand."

Eric asked, "Where is your brother?"

Vanessa answered, "In his room pretending to be at magic school."

Eric said, "Magic school… I guess it's good he has a big imagination because I'm not sending either of you there, at least not until college, and that is still a big maybe."

Vanessa with excitement in her voice remarked, "Wait, what? There are magic schools like in kids' books?"

Eric said, "Yes, but unlike the fantasy stories you read about in books, real magic schools are terrible. Anyway, both of you go and get your breakfast. That includes you, Willow. I know you ran over because Vanessa screamed. She is fine, and you need food if we are going to start more magic practice."

Willow told them she would meet everyone in the dining room in a few minutes. As Willow headed back to her room she wondered when her uncle noticed her. She also questioned if she could make it through breakfast.

As Willow forced herself to swallow the last of her grits, Pete said to his father, "Magic school can't be that bad."

Eric replied, "It is in this realm. All magic schools are like extreme military boarding schools in our realm. You have to work hard not just for good grades, but to survive."

With disbelief in his voice, Pete said, "Seriously?"

"Yes, when my parents sent me to magic school, they forced Felicia to send your Uncle Thomas with me."

"Why?"

"Wealthy magic families often send their staff's children to magic schools, under false pretenses of it being a scholarship opportunity. In reality, the servant's child is there to protect the wealthier child."

Felicia walked in and gave Eric a paper. As he read it, she said, "It's a disgusting practice."

She looked at Pete as she continued to say, "It would have been more beneficial to home school them both, instead of sending them to a place where they would end up having to spend money on therapists to deal with PTSD. Your grandfather was obsessed with your father going to Herschel Academy. It was the new, so-called prestigious school. The school was only six years old at the time and only three of its students survived to see graduation."

Pete sank in his chair as he said, "I don't want to go to magic school ever."

Felicia said, "I know what I said sounds scary; however, magic colleges are a whole different experience."

"Why?" asked Vanessa.

Eric answered, "Simple. The colleges can't afford to lose students. Only so many students survive magic schools, so colleges don't have a large crop to pick from."

Luna, who was cutting a runny egg, said, "I don't understand. Why are your magic schools determined to kill their students?"

Eric answered, "There is a fear that one day there will be another multi realm war. The schools feel that they need their students ready to fight an apocalyptic battle."

Willow said, "Why does every magic school in this realm feel that way?"

Martha said, "We can worry about that and the realms later. We don't have much time. Willow, let's start your magic defense training."

Luna asked, "Miss Martha, why do you feel we don't have a lot of time to train Willow?"

Martha said, "The curse on me is grow growing."

Willow noticed that her aunt had not taken a bite of her food. She started to ask if something was wrong when she suddenly felt something grab her. This caused her to jump up, but there was no one behind her. Willow said, "I just had a…"

Felicia suddenly appeared in front of her and started shouting a bunch of words Willow didn't understand. Thin golden chains appeared in front of her and quickly wrapped tightly around her. Sandy shouted, "Don't worry, we won't let you get taken!"

Vanessa shouted, "MOMMY, NO!!"

Willow turned her head in her aunt's direction. Martha cried, "We are out of time."

She started to fade as Eric was pointing a green staff at Martha. He started shouting as gold chains sprouted from the staff and wrapped around Martha. Willow was hit with a strange weightless sensation that caused her to fall to her knees. Eric stretched out his left hand and gold chains emerged from his palm and wrapped around Willow.

Martha shouted, "Your binding spells are useless. We are get, get, getting pulled back. Follow the magic trace we leave behind."

Suddenly Martha vanished in a flash of bright light. Eric shouted, "NO!" as his children screamed.

Luna, who had sprouted her wings, flew over to where Martha once stood and said, "We can find her, just focus on Willow."

Suddenly Willow found herself encircled in a bright white light. She could hear everyone shouting for a moment, but their voices soon faded away. Before Willow could even think about what was happening, the light was gone. She then found herself standing in front of a small run-down house in the middle of the woods. The house, with peeling white paint, a green door, and a lack of windows, stood in stark contrast to its surroundings.

Startled by what happened, Willow started to scream, and her aunt suddenly ran up to her. Martha quickly covered Willows mouth. She whispered, "Follow me." Then the pair ran into the woods. They ran as quickly as they could. As Willow felt sweat pouring down her face, her legs were getting so sore that she felt that she couldn't run for much longer. Martha stopped running. Willow almost fell to her knees as she panted heavily trying to catch her breath.

Martha said "Fuck, that son of a bitch really did it. He knew how to force us back here. But how did he figure it out? Dammit, I can't even portal us back."

Willow asked, "Auntie, what is going on?"

In a somewhat sarcastic tone Martha said, "Welcome to Texas, Willow. That house you saw is where we used to live. Before you ask, it doesn't have windows because I made it with magic, and I suck at making windows."

"How did we end up here so suddenly?"

Martha, attempting to explain, said, "The curse he put on me was complicated. I couldn't speak freely about anything that happened before we arrived in San Francisco unless I was four miles from our old house. I could not use my full power unless I was four miles from the house, and I can also only teleport us away from here one time. Unless the demon who cursed me dies, I can't open a portal to take us home. I teleported years ago to San Francisco, so until I kill that thing, I can't teleport again."

Confused, Willow questioned, "A demon did what?"

Martha suddenly sprouted pink and green fairy wings. She snapped her right hand and a white staff suddenly appeared in her hand. Martha said, "His name is Hayback, and he is a demon who possesses great power. He is one of the reasons we had to flee to this realm, and he is the one who cursed me.

When we first came here, I thought we had escaped him. I used my powers to make us a house, and we stayed here while I tried to think of a plan of what to do. Then he showed up. I won the fight, but he was able to curse me. I was too weak to finish him so I bound him to these woods and teleported us as far away as I could."

Suddenly they heard a man say, "Lady Havoc, why did you run?"

A man started to materialize in front of them. Martha pointed her staff at him as the man became more solid. The man had plaster white skin, long snow-white hair, silver eyes, and strange circular black markings all over his face. He was wearing a light blue tunic and brown pants with no shoes.

The man smiles at Martha as he said, "Lady Havoc, it's been ages. I haven't seen you since you failed to kill me. Oh, is that Little Monsoon? She really has grown."

Martha shouted, "Willow get behind me!"

Without a second thought, Willow got behind Martha. Martha did not take her eyes off the man, and she kept her staff pointed at him.

Shaky, Willow whispered as she asked, "Did he just call me Monsoon?"

Martha said, "That's not your name. My parents and my sister's ex-husband tried to make it your name. They failed, and your name is Willow."

The man smiled as he said, "That's not true. Lady Havoc, you raised your niece to be ashamed of her own name. That is just too cruel. But that doesn't matter. I'll be taking her magic now."

Martha snapped, "The fuck you will. How did you find us?"

The man replied, "A kind soul arrived to visit with knowledge of where the two of you were hiding. At first, she was not too willing to tell me where you were, believing that old myth to never make a deal with a demon nonsense. But after a number of trolls failed her, she accepted I was the better option."

Willow fell to her knees as she thought *Yennifer planned this. This is how she is going to kill us. I don't want to die; I don't want to die.*

Tears fell down Willow's face. Martha said, "Willow, don't worry. We bought a little time when we ran. The others should be able to trace us and teleport here."

At the news that help was on the way, Willow was able to regain her composure. As she got back on her feet, Hayback said, "Lady Havoc, don't lie to the girl."

Martha snapped, "Hayback, you know bringing me here weakens the curse you put on me. Remember the last time I could kick your ass on my own and escaped. What makes you confident about me losing to you this time?"

Hayback laughed as he said, "I have help this time."

Willow thought, *Yennifer.*

Suddenly she felt something wrap around her legs then drag her across the forest floor. Martha started to cast a spell to stop Willow from being dragged, but Hayback appeared next to her. He roundhouse kicked her into a nearby tree.

Martha coughed up blood as Willow found herself suddenly suspended in the air. Willow made futile efforts to shake herself free, and suddenly she was flung to the ground.

Yennifer walked up to Willow chuckling, "Time to get rid of the trash."

She shouted a spell and just as quickly, Willow screamed, "Relimaw!"

Instantly Yennifer was engulfed in blue flames. Yennifer began screaming, and Willow looked for her aunt. Willow soon picked up on the sound of her aunt shouting and headed in the direction of her voice. Her heart raced as she stumbled upon Martha being slammed into the ground by Hayback. Willow quickly looked around for anything she could use to fight Hayback. She spotted a rock and without a second thought she threw it at him.

The rock hit Hayback in the arm, causing him to lose his grip on Martha. Martha freed herself and then used her staff to hit Hayback with a ball of green light. When the light hit Hayback, he flew backwards. As he hit the ground, Martha raised her staff as if to make a final strike. It looked like Martha was about to cast a spell, but she paused for a second before lowering her staff. Martha closed her eyes and turned her head a little bit as if she were listening for something. As Willow questioned what her aunt was doing, Martha suddenly opened her eyes. Martha snapped, "There you are, bitch." Before Willow could blink, Martha sent a ball of red light in her direction. The ball of light flew past Willow, and she heard Yennifer scream.

Willow looked behind her as she saw Yennifer entangled in what looked like a glowing red net. The net was quickly swinging her around. Willow thought Yennifer was going to get sick when it slammed her to the ground and seemed to pin her there. Willow could tell that part of Yennifer's face looked burned; however, she was perplexed as to why only part of Yennifer's face was burned. She had seen Yennifer completely engulfed in blue fire.

Willow had little time to speculate about Yennifer's condition. Hayback was back on his feet. He and Martha were interlocked in an intense battle, shooting different spells at each other. Several times Martha attempted to hit Hayback with her staff, but he was able to block her attack with some kind of shield spell. As the battle raged on, Willow thought, *I must do something. But I don't know how to summon the fire again. Forget that. I don't even know how to control it. Wait, let me see if I can find some more rocks. I can hit him with them and maybe that will help auntie land a hit on that asshole.*

Willow started to look for rocks when she heard a loud clicking noise. A strange symbol that looked like a snake with horns appeared in the sky. In unison, Martha and Hayback yelled, "Fuck!"

Two large yellow trolls fell from the symbol and landed in front of Willow. Willow ran as fast as her legs could carry her. Sadly, the trolls were faster and one of them grabbed Willow. She screamed and kicked, demanding to be let go.

Willow heard Yennifer shout, "Serves you right, brat! One of you trolls get me out of this, then crush her. The troll holding Willow laughed. He said, "I don't take orders from you. Besides, your deal with my king was void as soon as you started working with that demon."

Yennifer began screaming all sorts of profanities. Meanwhile the troll holding Willow turned its attention to her. Willow, who was still struggling to get free wondered if she could summon fire again. The troll laughed as he said, "It's good we showed up when we did. She's a bigger prize than that damn princess."

The other troll replied, "Aren't we supposed to grab the princess, too?"

"Well yeah, but she's not here. This chick is, and we were supposed to take her anyway."

"Oh, I see. Should we head back?"

"I guess we can leav…"

Martha used her magic to slice the hand of the troll holding Willow. Willow landed on the ground hard. As she slowly stood up, she noticed that some of the troll blood had gotten on her clothes.

She looked at her aunt who was bloody and bruised. Martha snapped, "Willow what are you standing around for? Ru…"

Hayback appeared behind Martha. He conjured a red whip which he used to hit Martha in the head, making her fall. He then slammed his foot into her face, and she passed out. Willow started to run as the demon turned his attention to the trolls. He saw the troll that had Willow on the ground screaming as blood spewed from his severed hand. The other troll looked as if he did not know what to do next. Hayback frowned as he said, "I can't believe that the great demon that I am was really about to lose the girl to these weaklings."

The uninjured troll who seemed confused a moment ago collected his senses. He lunged toward Hayback. The demon, who seemed not to want to be bothered with the trolls, waved his hand. Instantly both trolls turned into confetti. Willow, who was running as fast as her legs could carry her, wondered if she could even escape. At the same time, she felt bad about running away when her aunt was hurt. Willow knew there was nothing she could do to help her aunt, but at the same time she felt that she just left her to die. Willow bumped into something hard that caused her to fall back. When she looked to see what she bumped into, her heart dropped. Hayback stood smiling in front of her. He said, "When I saw that symbol the trolls used to teleport here, I thought I was about to have to fight some high-ranking troll warriors. Lucky for me those were just a few grunts who thankfully distracted Lady Havoc long enough for me to knock her out. Sadly, most trolls are not that stupid. I am sure most likely more are on the way, and those two probably just arrived first. Monsoon, Willow, whatever the fuck you call yourself, I'm tired of hunting you. When Lady Havoc ruined my plan to steal you the first time, my boss was pissed.

When your aunt stopped me from capturing you a second time, my boss got angry. This is my last chance to capture you. My boss won't tolerate another failure. So, why don't you be a good girl and come with me without complaint? If you do, I won't kill Lady Havoc, and I really, really want to kill that bitch."

Willow, with fury in her voice, said, "Don't call my aunt a bitch, you piece of shit!"

Hayback replied, "If you know what's good for you, you'll shut the fuck up and come with me. I'm not weak like that woman you used that repel spell on. You won't be able to take me down so easily."

Willow thought, *what do I do? I can't fight him. But if I go with him, I know something bad will happen.*

Hayback snapped, "Stop wasting my time. Let's go!"

Suddenly Martha appeared, and she blasted Hayback with a ball of blue light. When the light hit him, he flew back. Hayback landed on the ground motionless. Martha fell to her knees while breathing heavily. Willow moved over to her aunt to see if she was alright. It was then she noticed that Martha's head was bleeding. Willow said, "Auntie, just rest. I'll run over to the house to see if there are any bandages."

Martha replied, "Don't bother. I already know there aren't any bandages, or anything else we can use. The others will probably figure out where we are soon anyway."

Martha looked at Hayback who still was not moving. She said, "I wish I had the power to finish off that demon."

Willow said, "I thought he was dead."

"I wish. It's hard to tell if a demon is dead because they don't breathe. I sense magic from him, so he is still alive."

"Is there a spell I can use to take him out? I have fairy and dragon powers and I should be able to use them."

"Dragon? Who told you, you have dragon magic?"

"Uncle said he tested my magic when I was little, and I have dragon magic."

Martha said, "Willow, he's wrong. You don't have dragon magic. But I see how he could make that mistake. You're part fairy, a little witch, but your witch magic is weak and not worth your time. That does not matter because you're predominantly a phoenix. That's why that demon was after you."

"Wow, I'm an actual phoenix magic type?"

"Yes, it's a power rarer than the dragon. Phoenix magic can be mistaken for dragon."

With concern in her voice, Willow said, "As much as I would like to learn more, should we do anything about that demon?"

"My magic is too weak. You need to practice with your magic for a while before you use it offensively. Otherwise, you might unintentionally start the biggest wildfire this country has ever seen."

"Well, the fire in the park was bad, but it wasn't that bad."

"That's because it was the first time you used magic. When you use magic the first time it won't come out at full force. After that, if you don't practice your magic, it can easily spiral out of control."

"Ok, but Hayback may wake up at any moment."

"True, but I sense Felicia's magic. It's weak but I can tell she's teleporting here, which means your uncle and the others will be here soon. When they get here, they can kill Hayback and that will free me from most of the curse."

"Why won't you be completely free?"

Martha explained, "Hayback is not the only one who put a curse on me. I promise to explain it all when we get home. There is so much I've wanted to tell you and show you."

There was a sudden cracking sound and Felicia appeared in front of them. Felicia said, "Thank goodness you're alright."

Martha said, "Felicia, quickly dispose of that demon."

Felicia looked at Hayback for a moment. She said a spell that sounded like she was saying the words backwards. Hayback burst into green flames. Both Martha and Willow took a breath of relief as he burned away.

Once his remains were ash, Felicia said, "Something does not feel right. Let's not find out what it is. I'm opening a portal and taking us home now."

"Felicia, where is Eric? I'm surprised he's not with you."

Felicia started to make a circular motion with her hands as she said, "We have a problem with the council. That's why it took longer than it should have to get here. I should have the portal open in a second. I'll send a council member here to pick up the baggage."

"Baggage?" asked Willow.

Felicia answered, "I'm talking about Yennifer. Since the council felt entitled to hold up everyone coming to your aid, I feel they should be responsible for picking her up."

A portal opened up, and Willow saw Eric and Sandy talking to people wearing red robes. Willow helped her aunt stand. Supporting her aunt with Willow's arms around her waist, the two of them walked toward the portal. Willow did not want to meet the people in red robes; however, she did not want to stay where she was either.

When they were close someone screamed, "No!" Then Willow felt ropes grab her from behind. Martha tried to hold onto her, but her efforts were futile.

Willow could see her aunt scream while Felicia tried to cast some kind of spell. Willow hit the ground only to find herself in strange surroundings. The sky was dark purple, and the sun was lime green. She appeared to be in a strange forest. All the plants were dark blue and red, except for the trees, which were striped orange and yellow. Before Willow could think, something grabbed her and threw her in a cart.

The door slammed as Willow stood up. It was then she saw two demons that looked like Hayback. The only difference is one demon did not have the markings on his face. The other demon had red markings instead of black ones. The demon with no markings said, "Stupid Hayback. I knew if we waited, we could grab the girl when no one was looking."

The other demon said, "Qeme, you're just lucky that I'm good at listening through a portal. You're also lucky I was willing to help. My time is important."

Qeme said, "Whatever, Lofen. I'm going to pay you as soon as we get back."

"I could wait for my pay or..."

Lofen pulled out a glowing red dagger and then stabbed Qeme. As Qeme faded into ash, Lofen began pulling the wagon that contained the cage which was holding Willow hostage. Willow asked, "Where are you taking me?"

Lofen answered, "Shut up, Bitch. I'm not wasting time talking to a human. Come tomorrow you're the boss's property anyway."

Willow sat in the cage as tears fell from her eyes.

Chapter 11

Demons

Willow was thrown into a cell. The cell had metal bars and a rock floor made of blue stone. The light in the area was dim, making it difficult for Willow to see clearly. Lofen laughed as he walked away. Willow curled up, feeling completely hopeless. More tears fell from her face as she gave up hope of going home.

She heard a voice say, "Hey, hey, kid come here."

Willow stood up and noticed the cell across from hers. There was a man with dark brown skin and a muscular build. His hair was black with a small patch of grey hair on the left side of his head. He had brown eyes and a small scar on his right cheek. He was wearing what looked like a blue robe. That reminded Willow of the type of robe wizards wore in movies. He also wore gray pants and thick brown leather boots.

The man asked, "What's your name, kid?"

In a tearful voice she replied, "It's Willow, sir."

"Willow, Willow. That's a nice name. My grandmother was named Willow."

"Oh um, that's interesting."

"My name is Lemarcus. Willow, are you a fast runner?"

"Um why ar…"

"Good, good because I've got a plan to get us out of here; I've got to get back to the rebel camp before sundown. Otherwise, they will send a team to get me. My wife has been captured by the enemy.

If the extraction team comes here, then that's risking manpower that I need to save my wife."

"I'm a little confused about what you..."

"Are you from this realm?"

"No, a demon pulled me through a portal and then locked me up here. Can you help me get home?"

Lemarcus replied, "Good, well not good that you are in this realm. Just good you're not from here. Sadly, I can't help you to return to your own realm right away. You will have to wait a few weeks."

Willow questioned, "Hold on just a moment please. Why do I have to wait to go home?"

"I'll explain as soon we get out of here."

"Ok, what do we have to do?

"Just follow me as I run out of here."

"Follow you?"

Lemarcus said, "For the most part yes. When we get out of the cells, I'll give you a flash plum."

"What is a flash plum?"

"It's a fruit that generates a bright light. It blinds a person for three seconds. When a demon encounters a flash plum the light kills them. The exits to this place are crawling with guards. When you throw the flash plum, it will kill the majority of the demons. After you throw the plum, we will have five minutes to escape. That is more than enough time to get to the nearby forest."

Willow, in a hushed tone, replied, "I guess that will work."

Lemarcus began making zig zag motions with his hands. When he stopped, the bars of his cell fell down in sliced pieces. As they hit the ground there was no sound. He repeated the motion and the bars of Willow's cell fell the same way. They both walked out of their cells.

Lemarcus handed Willow a glowing purple plum. He then conjured a ball of light, that to Willow resembled a small version of the sun.

Lemarcus said, "I'm going to throw this. When I do, we have to run."

Willow said, "Wait what if there are other people here?"

Lemarcus reassuring her said, "Don't worry. We are the only prisoners here. You probably didn't notice there are only two cells."

He then threw the ball down the hall behind them. Lemarcus shouted "Run!"

They dashed down the hall as there was a massive explosion. They kept running for a few minutes then raced down another hallway. They navigated a few corridors until they reached a flight of stairs. As they raced up the staircase, Willow could hear screaming. Lemarcus said, "Looks like that sun fire spell is still giving those devils trouble. If you don't know that spell, I'll teach it to you. It comes in handy when dealing with demons."

Willow asked, "Is it a hard spell?"

"No, it's pretty simple."

Willow, with a smile on her face, replied, "I can't wait to learn."

When they reached the top of the stairs Lemarcus motioned for her to wait. He peeped his head around the corner for a moment. Lemarcus whispered, "We are near the exit. There are a few demons near the exit. I'll engage them. When I do, I want you to head for the exit and throw the flash plum. Then run and when you get outside, hide in the forest. Don't worry. I will find you."

For some reason the moment Lemarcus said he would find Willow, her fear disappeared. Willow wondered why this stranger's promise made her feel better. She didn't know him, so why should she be so trusting of him?

Lemarcus conjured two orbs of blue light. He thew them at the demons who dodged both light orbs. The orbs exploded, and the demons started to chase Lemarcus who ran down the hallway. Once they were gone, Willow ran in the opposite direction. She soon saw several demons standing in the hallway. As soon as they noticed her, she threw the flash plum. The moment it hit the ground a bright light filled the hallway. Willow was forced to close her eyes as she heard the demon's scream. A moment later Willow opened her eyes. All the demons were gone. Without a second thought she ran outside.

Willow kept running until she reached the forest. She continued to run until her legs gave out and she fell. Soon after she hit the ground, she forced herself to get back up. She started to wonder how long it would take Lemarcus to get there.

As she sat there waiting, looking around, one thing was clear to Willow. She did not like this realm. All the plants were too odd, and looking at the sky made her feel uncomfortable. After a short time, Lemarcus arrived as promised. He sat across from her and said "Alright, here is the problem. As I said, I have to go back to the rebel camp. The rebel camp is on Dominnight G 428. Since I have to do that, it will be a few weeks before I can send you home. Opening portals to other realms without a license uses a massive amount of magic power."

Willow asked, "I thought you had to have a license to travel through the realms?"

"That's the lie the council tells so they can track people. I choose to traverse the realms without my license. It keeps the council from tracking me."

Willow thought, *there is an earth council and a multiverse council. Both are evil and there is a war going on that I know barely anything about. All this is giving me a fucking headache.*

Lemarcus smiled and said, "From the look on your face I'm guessing the multiverse and magic is bothering you."

"Yes, I just learned about all this multiverse and magic mess a few days ago. Then there are all these governments and laws I have to know about. Plus, I'm being attacked by demons and trolls because apparently, I'm a phoenix…"

Lemarcus corrected Willow, "You have phoenix magic?"

"Yes."

Lemarcus said, "Keep that information to yourself. Phoenix magic is extremely rare and powerful. The fewer humans or monsters that know, the better."

"Thanks, I didn't realize that. I'm just overwhelmed. I was about to return to my home when that demon grabbed me."

With sympathy in his voice, Lemarcus said, "I'm sorry you're going through this, kid. When we get to the camp, and you can get some rest you'll feel a little bit better."

Lemarcus clapped his hands together and as he slowly opened them, a portal appeared. On the other side was a camp with several people wearing robes like the one Lemarcus wore. There was nice green grass and a clear blue sky. Willow walked through the portal followed by Lemarcus.

Some people paused while others ran past Willow to greet Lemarcus. Willow almost fell when another woman caught her. The woman looked around the same age as Willow. She had smooth bronze skin and yellow eyes like a cat. Her dark brown hair had streaks of blue while her hair was styled in a large braid. She was wearing a blue witch robe with brown pants and gray boots. The woman asked, "Are you alright?"

"I'm ok," replied Willow.

"My name is Blossom. What's your name?"

"Willow."

Blossom said, "It's a pleasure to meet you, Willow. I can see you're new here. Why don't you come with me. I'll help you get settled. Don't worry about Lemarcus. He'll find you once his well-wishers settle down."

With a little hesitation in her voice Willow agreed saying, "Um ok."

Willow followed Blossom through the camp. They reached a large gray tent and went inside. The inside of the tent was larger than the outside. The tent looked like a windowless cabin, complete with wood floors and walls, and a wooden cabinet with a white countertop and sink on and against the leftmost wall. There was a fireplace in the back, a large round table in the center, and a large messy king size bed on the right side of the room. Blossom and Willow sat down at the table.

Blossom said, "Would you like some tea?"

"Sure, thank you," replied Willow.

Blossom got up and retrieved a stainless-steel teapot. After filling it with water, she hung the teapot in the fireplace. Blossom snapped her fingers, and a fire magically appeared. She then asked, "Where are you from?"

Willow answered, "I'm from Earth C157."

Blossom, providing information, remarked, "You probably already know that Lemarcus's wife has been taken. If we did not have to use all our resources to get her back, then Lemarcus would have sent you home."

"He mentioned that. So, did the demons kidnap him, too?"

"No, he went to realm LV3459 because there were rumors of the demons getting ahold of some kind of new power. I have no idea what it was or what that meant. I think Lemarcus feared the demons would launch another attack when we try to rescue his wife."

Willow thought *that is the place Luna mentioned to her where the war was being fought.*

"I understand, but I wish I could let my family know where I am."

"That won't be a problem. I can't send you home, but I can send a message to your home. Your loved ones will know you're safe."

"Thank you."

Blossom told Willow she would be back in a few minutes. Shortly after she left, Lemarcus came into the tent. He said, "Sorry about the mob rush when we arrived."

Willow said, "It's alright. I think I'm feeling a little better now that I'm out of demon world."

"Demon world is a good name for that place."

"Blossom told me you went there because the demons had some kind of weapon?"

Lemarcus, avoiding eye contact with Willow, answered, "Yeah, that turned out to be false information, but I'm glad I fell for it since you needed someone to help you get out of there."

Smiling, Willow said, "Thank you for saving me."

"No problem."

Blossom came back holding a crystal ball on a gold stand. She placed it on the table before going to check on the teapot. Lemarcus said, "Thank you, Blossom. We need to notify Willow's family about where she is."

Blossom said, "I agree, sir."

Lemarcus asked, "Willow, which realm are you from? Also, tell me the first and last names of your parents."

Willow answered, "I'm from Earth C157, and I live with my Aunt Martha Jones."

Lemarcus paused for a moment and then asked, "Your aunt's name is Martha Jones?"

"Yes."

Lemarcus said, "Um, alright."

Lemarcus waved his hand over the globe. It glowed with a bright white for a moment before turning black and making a buzzing sound."

Lemarcus hit the table and said, "Dammit."

Willow asked, "What happened?"

"I'm guessing Earth C157 is believed to not have magic wielders according to the multiverse council. Clearly Earth C157 likes it that way. That demon grabbing you and those trolls you dealt with must have caused a panic. They have put up a zone out for all communication to that realm, which means all secret methods of communicating with Earth C157 will be shut down for a month. This also will block all travel in and out of Earth C157 for four months."

Willows heart jumped. She thought *four months! Today just keeps getting worse. What am I supposed to do?*

Lemarcus took a breath before saying, "Blossom, can you give Willow and I a moment?"

Blossom said, "Sure," then left the tent.

"Is something wrong?" asked Willow.

"No, I need to ask you something. I have a strong feeling your answer will be what I want to hear. I'm just a little nervous about hearing it."

"Why?"

"I told you a partial lie about why I got captured by the demons. It's because I'm scared to tell you the real reason why I was there. That's not the full truth. I don't want Blossom to know why I was there. Although she may be suspicious, I wanted to get you out of that realm so badly I wasn't sneaky when we arrived here."

"I don't understand."

"I know, I know I'm not making any sense right now. It's been a while since I've been this nervous."

Willow felt her heart race as she asked, "Why are you nervous?"

"Were you raised by your aunt?"

"How do you know that?"

"You said her name is Martha Jones?"

Willow felt herself start to shake as she asked, "Yes, I just told you that."

Lemarcus smiled as his eyes started to water. He wiped away his tears as he said, "I think you're…"

Suddenly a baby girl wearing only a diaper rushed into the tent. The little girl had a pudgy face and short black hair. She looked up at Willow with big brown eyes and a big smile, exposing she only had her two bottom front teeth.

The baby hugged Willow's leg and made a squawking noise. She was soon followed by another child who appeared to be around four years of age. The little girl's black hair was in several plaits with bunny clips on the ends. She was wearing a purple T-shirt with a dragonfly on it. The child wore blue jeans, and her feet were adorned with pink sneakers.

Willow stared down at both girls. She started to notice how both children looked similar to her. In that moment Willow's heart stopped. Lemarcus said, "Daniela, I told you to play outside the tent with Samira."

Daniela said, "Daddy, you were taking forever. I wanna play with big…"

Lemarcus said, "I have to have a big peoples talk with Willow. Go out and play with Samira. You can play with Willow if she feels like playing after I talk to her."

Lemarcus wiped away more tears as he grabbed Samira. He carried her out of the tent with Daniela following behind. When Lemarcus returned, he looked at Willow while saying, "There is a lot that we need to talk about."

A tearful Willow rushed over to Lemarcus. She hugged him as she thought *I finally found them.*

To Be Continued

Want to learn more about me and my books? You can find out on my social media.

YouTube: @madamcrystalbutterfly

TikTok: madamcrystalbytterfly777

Instagram: mcbutterfly777

Threads: mcbutterfly777

www.ingramcontent.com/pod-product-compliance
Lightning Source LLC
LaVergne TN
LVHW050645100826
845148LV00011B/1984

* 9 7 8 1 7 3 4 8 6 8 6 8 5 *